THE KILLINGS ON KERSIVAY

Kersivay has changed. A prison-hospital for psychopaths has now been established on this quiet Hebridean island and Peter Parsons flies there to interview the locals on their reactions to it.

Peter's work as a radio producer takes on a new angle when a sex offender escapes and Joanna Campbell—a loose woman—is found dead. Hers will not be the only death under investigation and Peter, experiencing black outs, calls into question his own actions. The locals are gripped by fear as the moors are shrouded in fog.

But nothing in Kersivay is as straightforward as it seems. A chameleon sits on a twig, and is camouflaged, guarding a well-hidden secret. . .

THE KILLINGS ON KERSIVAY

Angus MacVicar

M

First published 1962
by
John Long Ltd

This edition 2000 by Chivers Press
published by arrangement with
the author

ISBN 0 7540 8566 X

British Library Cataloguing in Publication Data available

Printed and bound in Great Britain by
Redwood Books, Trowbridge, Wiltshire

Contents

The Chameleon (*Chamaeleo, Daud.*) is a reptile belonging to the Saurian or lizard-like order. It possesses the remarkable power of changing its colour to correspond closely to that of the surface on which it rests. Frequently the camouflage is so perfect that it cannot be seen lying on a leaf or twig a few feet away. Under stress of fear or sexual disturbance, however, it is unable to maintain its assumed colour, and one can observe it slowly changing back to its natural hue.

BURFORD'S *Natural History*

1

Fog Over Kersivay

'WE'VE been working you too hard,' said Head of Features, twinkling like the Laughing Cavalier. 'The announcers have to read your name so often they're becoming nervous. "Produced by Peter Parsons" – too close to a tongue-twister for comfort.'

I agreed.

'And yet,' he said, consulting a tablet on his desk, 'and yet you're not due to go on leave until the end of October.'

I nodded. The date was September the fourteenth. Outside Broadcasting House the town was enjoying the fag-end of summer, its streets hot and raucous.

He changed direction. 'Didn't your people come from the island of Kersivay, in the Outer Hebrides?'

'I was born there. Went to the village school. But I haven't been back since my father died – almost twenty years ago. When I was nine.'

'Like to go back?'

His conversational drift finally made sense. 'Yes,' I said, cagily, and we smiled at each other.

'This prison they've built on your island,' he continued, 'it's causing a good deal of controversy. I believe there's a programme in it. Psychopaths are topical.'

'The authorities don't call it a prison,' I pointed

out. 'Officially it's a hospital for criminal loonies.'

'Exactly. Our psychiatrist would give his point of view. We might even persuade the Minister of Health to do a spiel – though I notice he does his best to shy clear of the subject nowadays. But the really interesting angle would be the reaction of the natives. Their views on having what you call "criminal loonies" parked on their doorsteps.'

'A series of on-the-spot recordings?' I suggested.

'Yes. Let's see.' He studied the tablet. 'The Derbyshire potters are due on the air on Tuesday. After that you have nothing on the stocks for three weeks. Can you leave on Wednesday?'

'Nothing to stop me. But I could make all the recordings necessary in a week.'

'Knowing your capacity for hard work, Peter, I'd say you could make all the recordings necessary in a couple of days. Take three weeks all the same. Leave your secretary behind and do the job by yourself. I'll see you get full expenses – and something over.'

'Thanks,' I said, and meant it.

'By the way,' he added, showing only a suspicion of embarrassment, 'how are things going? Getting over it?'

'Could be,' I said. 'This may help the cure.'

He smiled. 'That had occurred to me.'

A good old scout, the Laughing Cavalier.

As he had arranged, I disembarked from the Viscount at Renfrew and, along with eleven other passengers, boarded a Pionair for Kersivay. We flew out over the Firth of Clyde, its blue-green beauty reminding me of a Disney film, then soared higher to avoid updraughts from the craggy mountains of

Argyll. Half an hour later we were floating in a clear sky four thousand feet above the Minch. Sapphire blue and wrinkled, it was entirely empty except for one small steamer with a black and red funnel which crawled out on a white wake towards the Hebrides.

On the seat beside me lay my midget tape-recorder, a solid link with reality; but now a tune came into my head – *'Speed bonny boat like a bird on the wing'* – and the dismay and depression of the past year were momentarily submerged in an effervescence of good spirits.

I had a look at my fellow passengers.

They included a young matron, surrounded by parcels and three small children, whose rosy complexion marked her as a native of Kersivay returning from a shopping spree in Glasgow; two young farmers, each with a shepherd's crook, immersed in amiable argument about a recent sale of black-faced lambs in Oban; a mature and portly couple, almost certainly man and wife, who seemed to be making a late holiday trip to the island; two commercial travellers exchanging 'shop' on the subject of soap powder – and finally, across the passage from where I sat, a lean, tall, middle-aged man, immaculately tweed-suited, whose occupation I couldn't even guess at. But I noticed three gaily coloured fish-hooks in the band of his Donegal hat, and it occurred to me that his brown face and sleepy brown eyes were somehow familiar.

Minutes passed. Shyly smiling, the young matron convoyed her brood to the lavatory aft. The stewardess came round with barley sugar. The engine droned, and the sun beat on the Pionair's ports. On the horizon ahead the grey-blue hills of Kersivay emerged slowly from the Atlantic.

Metaphorical gears clicked in my head. I found I could remember.

The little school, its class-room smelling of peat-smoke, its playground filled with hens and gulls quarrelling for crusts from our midday 'pieces', their squawking terrifyingly loud to a small boy of nine. The teacher, young Murdo Cameron, tall and glossily dark, shouting fierce instructions as he taught us how to play shinty. Nappy Neil, my special pal – he'd been the shinty star, wielding his small *caman* left-handed and striking the ball with the hard accuracy of most *cioteachs.*

Nappy Neil MacDonald. I smiled to myself, picturing his narrow, freckled face. Bare-skuddy, we'd bathed together from the white beach below the hotel; we'd guddled for trout in the hazel-bordered burn in *Gleann nan Taibhis,* the Glen of the Ghost; up on the shoulder of Unival we'd searched for peewits' eggs. He'd protected me from potential bullies. He'd made me helpless with laughter at his famous impersonation of a waddling duck, which also so wickedly resembled the gait of old Annie Mary McCuish, the shop. A great man, Nappy Neil. At the time he'd been ten years old.

Other faces and memories were less distinct. Willie Ross, hard and strong, a great exponent of the art of hammer-throwing: he'd been known to everyone as the King of Kersivay, because he served on the County Council and owned the hotel and farmed a wide tract of land which bordered ours. Roderick MacLeod – Roderick Dhu – who'd been our gardener, a dark and terrifying throw-back to the Picts, though his wife, my mother's maid, had been extrovert and kind. Sandy Fraser, the blue-guernseyed fisherman, whose hands always looked as if they'd just come out of the cold sea. Maggie McDiarmid, the post office. Old Dr Graham.

Recollection of Dr Graham brought to the surface a different set of memories. The Big House, where I'd stayed with my parents, its lawns and flower-borders in startling contrast to the dun-coloured moorland round about. My father with his stick and pain-racked, patient face, suffering from a war wound and dying at last of its effects. The fuss and turmoil as my mother and I left Kersivay, the Big House sold and empty, the furniture packed in the hold of the steamer – a steamer with a black and red funnel and a white wake like the froth on lemonade.

Now the pictures flickered faster, because I disliked the look of them. The dry old solicitor, monocled and white bearded, speaking gravely to my mother as I clung to her hand in his office. Her face, pale but smiling, when she told me I'd have to go to boarding-school, because most of the money my father had earned as a writer had been lost in a badly chosen investment, making it necessary for her to begin work as a business-man's secretary. Her face, flushed and happy, after her marriage to the business man, while I stood on the steps of the hotel, ten years old, tightly shod and miserable, waving them off on their honeymoon.

Broadcasting House. The picture-rate slowed down again. 'Brilliant young Peter Parsons,' the critics had said. But it wasn't brilliance – it was hard work and a Calvinistic attention to detail, as I well knew. However, I'd appreciated success, and a certain wariness in regard to friends and friendship had begun to disappear. A happy time, made happier when Myra took over a part in a dramatized documentary I was producing – about a doll-factory, of all things.

I glanced out of the port at my right elbow and saw a horizon-wide bank of fog rolling in towards Kersivay. In less than half an hour, I reckoned, it would engulf the sunlit island – in much the same way as Myra's departure with my assistant to Singapore had engulfed my existence, less than six months ago. She'd been living with him for weeks, I learned. She'd been living with him even at those times when I'd held her small, passionate body in my arms and it had seemed to me that we'd achieved a perfect accord, both spiritual and physical.

A small pain began to gather behind my eyes. I recognized the signs and with an effort mentally sidestepped that other, final memory – that memory which in reality was not a memory at all but a degrading suspicion – and transferred my thoughts to the present. It was the only way to preserve sanity and self-respect. Work, work, work. Think of the present, Parsons. And of the future, if you dare.

The drone of the engines changed pitch, and an illuminated sign warned us to stop smoking and fasten our safety-belts. The stewardess emerged from the flight-deck, trim and smiling. 'We'll get down before the fog comes in,' she promised.

Fumbling with a buckle, the lean man glanced in my direction. 'Thought for a minute we weren't going to make it. This your first trip to Kersivay?'

'No. I used to live here. What about yourself? Going fishing?'

'That's right.' His smile was oddly secretive, his

accent difficult to place. 'I'm staying at the hotel. With the King of Kersivay, as I believe he's called.'

'Willie Ross?'

'Yes. Do you know him?'

'I did. He must be almost seventy now. As a matter of fact I wondered if he were still alive. When my secretary wrote to book me in at the hotel it was someone called Rona Carmichael who answered.'

'Mr Ross's granddaughter. His right-hand woman, he says. Charming. Trained as a nurse in London before her mother died and she came back to help the old man.'

'So you've been to Kersivay before?'

'Once. About six weeks ago, at the beginning of August. I liked the place so much I decided to make a return visit. My name's Harringay, by the way. Kenneth Harringay.'

'But of course!' I said. 'At Broadcasting House we call you the fisherman-poet. I spoke to you once in the canteen.'

'On target,' he acknowledged, and for a moment his smile lost its cunning. 'Now let me try! You're Peter Parsons, the producer. On the evidence of that tape-recorder you're going to Kersivay to make a programme about the new prison.'

'It's a small world,' I said, heavily.

He nodded. 'And getting smaller.'

The pain still worried me, but I went on trying to ignore the cause of it.

We were circling now to make a landing, and the whole island lay below us like a large-scale model.

To the east the green hills of Unival and Hirsay were purple-patched with heather and dotted white by grazing sheep. Between them *Gleann nan Taibhis* looked dark and secretive in bird's-eye perspective; but the flooded burn emerging from it was bright in the sun. It ran down, sparkling, through the moor and machar-land, past isolated shepherds' cottages, past the Big House with its white-washed walls and banks of dull red fuchsia, past snug and prosperous-looking farmhouses, past the hydro-electric power house and the widely scattered grey village, finally meeting the sea in a rocky corner of the hotel's white beach. To the south, across fenced-in fields – yellow stubble-fields lately emptied of oats and barley, emerald pastures containing herds of cattle – there came into view a brick building of ultra-modern design, white-topped and many windowed. From photographs I had seen I recognized the prison. On three sides it was sheltered by a wood; but its pale, hygienic frontage faced the sea, and already the fog from the Atlantic was wisping up to the brick wall which surrounded it.

A lifting wing-tip obscured the place, and concrete runways appeared in front. As the Pionair levelled and eased down I saw a group of people and cars waiting outside the buff-coloured airport building.

Harringay smiled with one side of his mouth. He said: 'There's been some rain, I see. And this fog may bring more. The fishing ought to be good.'

I was surprised by the way he said it.

The Pionair touched down. As we disembarked we rubbed shoulders with passengers waiting to come aboard. Luggage, mail, newspapers, crates of bread and groceries were already being unloaded at speed, because the pilot was in a hurry to be off again. Fog had now blotted out completely the south-eastern tip of the island.

Gaelic talk floated on a tangy breeze which smelt of

salt and peat. Harringay recognized the hotel station-wagon and climbed in. I parked my tape-recorder at the back beside him, then stood at the door, lighting a cigarette while I waited for the driver to appear with the luggage.

He came across from the plane at last – wiry and freckled, sandy hair flying in the wind, long blue jersey tight around narrow hips. Having arranged our cases in the boot, he was about to get into the driving-seat when he saw me.

We stared at each other, and a sudden joyful recognition helped me in my struggle to forget. 'Nappy Neil!' I exclaimed.

'Peter!' His mouth opened, white teeth parting in a grin of delight. 'Man, I'm glad to see you! They told me about a Mr Parsons, but I never dreamt it would be you! How are you, eh? A great man on the wireless nowadays. But you have been ill, I was hearing?'

'I'm better now.' I continued to shake his hand. 'It's grand to be back – and grander still to be welcomed by Nappy Neil.'

He punched my chest. 'You're a bit thin and pale,' he told me, 'and those horn-rims make you look about a hundred. But och, we'll soon put that right in Kersivay! It'll be a holiday you're having?'

'In a way. I'll tell you later.'

I experienced an odd shift in perspective. For years I'd been the boss, chivvying young actors, encouraging technicians, bullying shy members of the public into brief flirtations with the microphone. Now those years were apparently as nothing. I was back in an old relationship, in which Nappy Neil performed the boss's role and I a secondary, dependent one.

We got into the station-wagon, still talking. I turned to Harringay, eager to introduce my boyhood friend, but it appeared they had met before, during the summer. Nappy Neil, I discovered, was boots, chauffeur and general handyman at the hotel.

True to form he was a dashing driver. The tyres whined as we sped out through the airport gates on the four-mile run to the hotel.

The Pionair cast a running shadow on the moor as it roared away above us, safely launched on its return journey. The pilot had taken off just in time. Half a minute later the fog surged in, blanketing the sun and extinguishing colour. Reluctantly Nappy Neil slowed down.

'Bad, bad!' he said, peering hawk-like through the damp windscreen. 'But we're used to fog in September. Tomorrow it will be gone.'

Ghost-like farm buildings swam past. Looming large as llamas, sheep scuttered away from under the bonnet.

Nappy Neil switched on a fog-light and chuckled to himself. 'Do you mind the time we got lost, Peter – on our way to harry gulls' nests on the Hirsay Cliff?'

'Do I not! When the fog cleared we were right on the edge, and I was sick looking down.'

'I was sick after the belting I had from the schoolmaster!'

'You took all the blame, Nappy Neil. I got off with a lecture. By the way, is Murdo Cameron still schoolmastering?'

'Ay, indeed. Grey in the head now, and not so spry at the shinty, but as ferocious as ever. He was mad when they built the prison. Writing letters to the papers, organizing protest-meetings. Man, he was in his element!'

'Was there much local opposition?' said Harringay from behind. 'To the prison, I mean.'

'Well, there was – and there wasn't. The building of it created a lot of well-paid employment. Now that it's in full operation, so to speak, the shopkeepers and the farmers are doing big business – groceries, milk, potatoes, all kinds of stuff. To begin with some people were afraid that one of the sex-murderers might escape, but you know how it is – when folks' pockets are well filled the rights and wrongs of a situation don't seem to matter; and in any case nothing has happened yet, and the Governor has promised that it never will. The warders and medical staff don't bother us much, either. They keep themselves to themselves.'

Drops of heavy rain oiled down the wind-screen. The fog became thicker, the day darker. As we passed a row of village houses and made a sharp turn to the right I heard a banshee wail which tortured the nerves in my head.

Nappy Neil must have noticed my reaction. 'It's the fog-horn on Cladach, Peter. Remember – underneath the lighthouse, where we used to spear flounders?'

I nodded.

'Another mile,' he said, risking a shade more of the accelerator. 'A good dram is what you need.'

Harringay leant forward, tapping his shoulder. 'Mr Parsons calls you Nappy Neil. An odd name, surely?'

He grinned. 'Blame my great-grandfather for that one! He and my great-grandmother were chewing the rag about what to call their only son – who was my grandfather of course. In the end my great-grandfather went off to the registrar – huffy as hell and muttering about obstinate women – and my great-grandmother screeched after him: "There's nothing obstinate about me. Call him Napoleon Bonaparte if you like!" And well – that's exactly what he did!'

Harringay laughed outright. 'But why should his descendants have to suffer?'

'Tradition, Mr Harringay. In the islands an eldest son is always called after his grandfather. To do otherwise would be a terrible insult to the whole family. In my case they left out the Bonaparte but stuck to Napoleon. I don't mind at all. It's very distinguished!'

With a flourish he halted the station-wagon outside the front door of the hotel. The railings flanking the wide steps dripped with moisture. It was dark and very still, except for the faraway sound of the foghorn.

2

Black-out

THE tall girl at the reception desk had thick black hair stylishly cut and blue eyes clear as a sea-pool. Her face was pale but healthily tanned. On account, perhaps, of the high, prominent cheek-bones, it hinted at a kind of sorrow – until she smiled. Then it became alive and beautiful. She wore a white blouse and narrow, navy blue skirt.

Her face was full of animation as she greeted Kenneth Harringay. But when she gave me the book to sign it betrayed only negative politeness. This, I gathered, was Rona Carmichael.

As advised by Nappy Neil, I had a dram and a couple of aspirins. Then I went upstairs to my bedroom, took off some of my clothes and lay beneath the quilt, determined to subdue the devils in my head. And in spite of the claustrophobic fog and the continuous wailing of the fog-horn, I slept for nearly an hour.

At seven o'clock I felt more relaxed and had a meal in the dining-room.

The lights were on, glowing warmly on murals depicting Kersivay sea-scapes. Dahlias bloomed close to the big bay windows, and I had a notion that though presently shrouded by the fog fertile lawns and gardens lay beyond them. The tables were only sparsely filled – by holiday-makers, I guessed. Harringay was not there, and it struck me as odd that he should have left the hotel on such a night. However, it was none of my business.

I sat by myself at a corner table and was served by a small, tartan-sashed waitress with rosy cheeks and the gentle voice of the islands, who kept smiling at me in a friendly way.

As she brought in the carageen and cream, I said: 'Are you from Kersivay yourself?'

'Indeed I am.' She hesitated, blushing a little; then it came out with a rush: 'Oh, Mr Parsons, Nappy Neil was telling me – about you and him being such old friends. You – you would be knowing my grandmother, I'm sure. Annie Mary McCuish, the shop.'

'Annie Mary! She made the best treacle-toffee in the world!'

'She is still alive, you know. But getting old and doddery. It's my mother who looks after the shop nowadays – and makes the treacle-toffee!'

'Then you're Katie – wee Katie McCuish. I was in the kirk the day you were christened.'

A stout lady at a near-by table – Lancastrian by her accent – demanded a jug of water. Katie supplied it, then returned to my side.

'Nappy Neil is always telling me about the ploys you used to have. He's so pleased that you are back.'

Her left hand strayed shyly on the tablecloth, and I noticed the ring with its three small diamonds. 'Katie,' I exclaimed, 'don't tell me—'

'Oh, it's true!' she said, her blush deepening. 'We got engaged just last week. We're being married in November, when the season is over.'

'Wonderful! Nappy Neil was always lucky!'

Another waitress came across and whispered. Katie nodded.

To me she said: 'You must excuse me, Mr Parsons – more people are coming in. Nappy Neil was saying maybe he'd see you in the bar after dinner.'

'Right, Katie. That's the plan.'

I tried hard to avoid comparing her innocence with Myra's ruthless sophistication; but half an hour later, when I entered the bar, my head had begun to throb again.

Nappy Neil was wearing a smart tweed jacket and flannel trousers. When he saw me he broke off his conversation with a big shirt-sleeved man on the opposite side of the counter and waved his tankard.

'Come away, Peter! Come and pay your respects to the King himself!' After his day's work, as is the way of the islands, he mixed on equal terms with his employer and the guests.

I shook hands, and Willie Ross's dour and craggy face underwent a change – a masculine version of what happened to his grand-daughter's expression when she smiled.

'Man, Peter, it's good to see you!' His voice was hoarse as I remembered it. 'Pity you've come back to Kersivay in a fog. Your mother now – what is the news about your mother?'

'I haven't seen her for some time. She married again.'

The King glanced at me, shrewdly. Then he leant powerful bare arms on the counter.

'Rona was telling me you have a tape-recorder in your luggage. Is it a programme you're after?'

I nodded. 'About the prison. What you folk think of it.'

'I see. Well, there's none of us what you might call radio stars, but I'm sure we'll all be glad to give you what help we can. Your father was a brave man – a good neighbour and a kindly laird.'

Nappy Neil grinned. 'Bring your recorder in here on a Saturday night, Peter. Then you'll get the truth. Murdo the schoolmaster – dead against it. Dr Barbour and the Major – all for it. With the King here, as County Councillor, trying to hold the balance. Sometimes I've seen Murdo and Dr Barbour on the verge of fighting, especially when the drams have been plentiful.'

I ordered a whisky and another pint for Nappy Neil. 'Dr Barbour – surely he's new since I left?'

'He's new,' agreed Willie Ross. 'About your own age. He took over when old Dr Graham retired to Oban about five years ago.'

'Modern,' said Nappy Neil, with an undertone of respect.

'And the Major?'

The King's face became dour again. 'Major Rivington-Keel. He bought the Big House and the estate from the old lady who took over from your mother. Soon after the war it was.'

'You've met his kind. Military God Almighty.' For once Nappy Neil wasn't smiling. 'But he was wounded in the face fighting for his country – and has plenty of money to spend – so we touch our bonnets and put up with him.'

'Now, now, lad – less of your Bolshie talk here!' Willie Ross's voice took on a regal edge of authority. 'He's a good enough laird and does his best to be affable. It's just his way.'

'Have you ever seen him kill a rabbit? He takes his time before he breaks its neck.'

One of the other half-dozen customers approached the counter to have his glass refilled.

The King prepared to serve him, but before he moved away he said: 'Anyway, Peter, have a good time while you're in Kersivay. Don't hesitate to ask Rona or me for anything you want.' His face lit up again. 'And if this rascal here invites you to go poaching on my stretch of the river in *Gleann nan Taibhis* – well, just look out if I catch you!'

Nappy Neil was laughing as he led me to a seat in a corner. 'That means if I *don't* take you poaching he'll not be pleased! He's a character, the King. Typical of Kersivay – saying one thing and meaning another.'

As I sat down pain stabbed at the roots of my eyes. The bar became a blur of glass and chrome and light-coloured wood. The low ceiling with its rank of strip-lights seemed to move down on top of me like an elevator. I gripped the edge of my chair and by an effort of will steadied myself. The smoke-haze stopped writhing.

'By the way,' I said, trying to sound casual, 'congratulations seem to be in order. Katie told me in the dining-room.'

He nodded. 'There's not many like Katie.' But as he said it he was eyeing me with concern, and I could see the knuckles of his left hand growing pale as his grip on the tankard tightened. 'Peter,' he went on abruptly, 'what's the matter?'

I wanted to tell him. He was the one friend to whom I could have spoken freely and without shame. I think I might have told him everything – even about the black-out and the terrifying days that had followed – but as I tried to collect my wits the door was pushed open. Out of the blackness a stream of fog entered the bar.

A man stood in the opening – tall, wiry and of middle-age, thick grey hair glinting with fog-damp, heavy walking-stick raised to attract attention. His deep-set eyes were angry.

'I knew it! I told them! And now it's happened!'

He came striding in and slammed the counter with his stick.

Nappy Neil sprang up. 'Murdo, man – what's got into you?'

And Willie Ross, glowering, caught the stick and held it firmly in one mighty hand. 'Out with it, Murdo! Tell us!'

Nappy Neil and some of the other customers gathered in a semi-circle close to the schoolmaster. His characteristic dark glossiness had turned to grey, but otherwise he hadn't changed so much.

'Tell us, Murdo!' repeated the King.

'I was in the shop. Buying cigarettes. Outside I bumped into Constable McKechnie, groping his way to the prison. One of their precious "patients" has escaped!'

The bar became silent. The pain in my head was so bad I wanted to go outside and be sick. But I waited.

'My God!' muttered Nappy Neil. 'When did it happen?'

'This afternoon, when the fog came down. But the damned fools didn't miss him until half an hour ago – at eight o'clock.'

'Then he's been on the loose for almost five hours?'

'Good for you, Nappy Neil! Fifteen years left school and you can still count!'

'Easy, Murdo!' Willie Ross kept hold of the stick. 'Which of them is it?'

'Terry Jackson, the Borstal boy from Nottingham. Raped a girl in a back alley and choked her to death. He had a black-out, they said. Poor Terry! You've got to think of poor Terry, and to hell with the womenfolk of Kersivay!'

I had begun to shiver. If I went out for a minute or two I could be sick in peace, and afterwards the cold fog might soothe the pain. I got up.

At a glass-topped table a young Cockney visitor sat with his girl-friend. He called out: 'What's being done about it? I mean, haven't they organized a search-party or something?'

Heavily, almost cumbrously, Willie Ross shook his head. 'No good in a fog like this, Mr Catford. But when it lifts they'll soon find him. He can't escape from Kersivay.'

As I made for the door I heard the schoolmaster's voice again, vehement and angry, giving more information. Terry Jackson, improving in health, had been given a job in the prison garden. He'd been weeding a rose-border when the fog had rolled in. Later, when he failed to answer the supper-bell, they'd found his deeply indented footprints on the soft turf outside and a piece of cloth torn from his shirt among the slivers of grass which topped the twenty-foot wall.

But at the moment I absorbed such details only subconsciously. My main concern was to get out into the open, away from this stifling place with its smell of smoke and spirits. No one noticed me leave. The sound of their excited, argumentative voices was cut off as I closed the door.

The fog surged round me in the dark. With a certainty that was half instinct, half a childhood memory, I crossed an asphalt yard and found the road to the village. I could hear nothing except the fog-horn, still wailing in the distance.

My toes encountered a grassy verge and I fell on my hands and knees. I tried to be sick and failed. I saw flashing lights, and it took me a few seconds to realize they were imaginary.

I caught part of a wire fence and tugged myself upright. With a vague idea of getting to the village and ringing the doctor's door-bell, I began to move along the road.

No longer did I try to ignore the devils swarming in for a final assault. I knew I was going to have a black-out; but it now occurred to me that if I got to this Dr Barbour before it happened, he might be able to help. Modern, Nappy Neil had called him.

I kept on, stumbling against the verge, wary about traffic which never materialized. The village was less than a mile from the hotel. I could reach it in twenty minutes if I hurried.

As time went on and the prospect of assistance loomed larger, I allowed the last of my memories to return.

It had happened two days after the final break with Myra.

I'd been drinking with Charles, one of the drama producers: drinking hard in a determined effort to alleviate spiritual and physical pain. Charles congratulated me on my escape – he'd known what had been going on, he said.

After he left to attend a rehearsal, my headache had grown steadily worse, and as I continued to brood over successive whiskies, erotic fancies had begun to crowd my brain. I'd wrestled with stubborn naked women and tried without success to have my will of them. They'd possessed Myra's face and body, and yet I'd known that none of them was Myra.

The pain had grown worse, my fancies more savage. I'd been sick in the lavatory of the pub. Then I'd gone out into the darkness of the city and the dream women screamed at me, and I'd gripped their throats to silence them. The last throat had been Myra's.

I'd come to myself in my own bed, in my own flat, and though my headache was gone and my body had a feeling of release, there was blood on my right hand – blood which came from no injury of mine.

I had told no one. For days I had read the papers and listened to the news bulletins with apprehension. For days I had dreaded a knock on the door which might herald an inquisition by the police. As far as I could tell, however, nothing had happened on the night of my black-out – at any rate in the district where I lived – and the police had never come.

But the fact remained that I couldn't account for several hours of my life – hours in which my hand had touched blood and subconscious fear had guided me home.

Some time afterwards I remembered that before going out to drink with Charles I had bought a piece of steak and put it in the refrigerator. Next day my char said its paper wrapping had been taken off – gremlins in the night, she had suggested. The thought gave me some comfort, but not much.

I had bought and borrowed many books on the subject of mental illness and had discovered that sexual frustration can, under certain circumstances, cause a violent headache followed by a black-out, during which a patient's moral responsibility may be temporarily abandoned. Relief is sometimes obtained by an act of sexual violence.

Now, moving forward in the darkness and the fog, I allowed long-suppressed anxieties full play. Was I in truth a psychopath, to be ranked beside Terry Jackson and other inmates of Kersivay's prison? Had I raped a woman – had I even killed a woman – on that occasion in the city? Was I capable of committing an involuntary act of violence in my native island?

I should have gone to a doctor long ago. He might have convinced me that my trouble was over-strain – or, in the event of a more serious diagnosis, suggested appropriate treatment. But I had been afraid that the probings of a psychiatrist might uncover some dreadful crime for which I would be blamed. I was still afraid, but this time I had made up my mind to submit myself to medical examination.

The stabs in my head were vicious now, and I had to close my eyes. This didn't make much difference, because in any event I could see only a foot or two in front. I had no erotic fancies, but I experienced a tension in all my muscles which struggled for release.

How long I continued in this way, stumbling, groping, only half aware of my physical surroundings, I had no means of telling. Even if I'd thought of looking at my wrist-watch its plain face would have been invisible in the dark.

It suddenly became apparent however, that the tarmac under my feet had changed to grass and heather.

The sour taste of panic came into my mouth. I was lost – perhaps on the moorland to the south, in the direction of the Big House. Had I subconsciously turned away from the doctor to seek a spurious comfort in my old home?

Slight rain mingled with the fog. I tripped on a low, broken-down stone wall and thrust out a hand to steady myself. It struck metal – a hollow-sounding metal, wet and rusty to the touch – and I knew exactly where I was.

Near the Hirsay Cliff, on the machar-land between the hotel and the prison, there had once flourished a small factory in which sea-weed was stored in great metal vats, later to be processed into a type of fabric. The building had been disused for years, and Nappy Neil and I had often played amongst the ruins, throwing stones at what remained of the vats.

I leant against the rusty metal. Instead of approaching the village I had been going in the opposite direction.

Lights were flashing again, and suddenly the moan of the fog-horn was being interrupted by other sounds.

They came to my blurred mind as if through a faulty radio receiver: a man's voice with a snarl in it like that of an angry animal; a woman's voice rising in pitch to words which sounded like '. . . *blackmail* . . . *nasty* . . . *barman* . . .' Then a scream, a scream of excruciating terror which ran through my head like a whirling saw.

I took out my handkerchief to wipe the sweat and dampness from my eyes. My cigarette-case came with it and fell against the wall.

I didn't try to look for it. At that moment the

scream occurred again, and I ran forward with the intention of finding and succouring a fellow-creature in distress.

But even as I ran, the pain and the lights and the darkness overwhelmed me. I had my black-out.

3

A Dying Fall

I CAME to myself, lying in a patch of bracken ten yards from the top of the Hirsay Cliff.

It was daylight, and the fog had gone. Two hundred feet below was the yellow beach, with white waves crawling at its edge, and the sea beyond stretching blue to the horizon. Gulls squabbled on the cliff, and the air was fresh with the scent of salt and wild thyme.

It sat up. The bracken was damp, my flannel suit was damp; but despite a tendency to shiver I had a sense of physical well-being. My headache had gone. My faculties were under control.

The sun warmed my back. Getting to my feet, I turned and saw it low above the Minch to the east, a ball of fire revitalizing the grey-green island. My wrist-watch showed the time to be six o'clock.

Desire for a cigarette made me fumble in my pocket for a case which wasn't there. Memory returned. So did fear.

Nothing stirred, except the gulls. I looked about me.

Far away to the left, under the summit of Unival, a gleam of concrete marked the airport. From there the dark ribbon of road wound past low-lying farms and through the straggling rows of village houses, flanked to the east by the squat grey chapel and to the west by the blunt spire of the parish kirk. Then it turned quickly towards the hotel and the red-roofed coastguards' cottages near the mouth of the river.

My eye followed the river back beyond the village and into dark *Gleann nan Taibhis*. Higher up on the moor I saw the whitewashed gables of the Big House and, farther to the right, behind a semi-circle of trees, the flat roofs of the prison. On the machar-land which rolled up from the cliff-top lay the gaunt ruin of the sea-weed factory, momentarily shadowed by the shoulder of Hirsay. It was less than three hundred yards from where I stood.

I made a calculation. For almost eight hours, it seemed, I had been unaware of my actions. What had happened in these eight hours? I examined my hands and clothes. They were dirty: that was all.

I began to walk towards the factory, not daring to admit, even to myself, that my intention was to look for something other than a cigarette-case. The exercise warmed me and took the stiffness from my muscles.

Within the crumbling stone wall half an acre of green turf was strewn with boulders and small stones, like a cake topped with currants and sultanas. The cracked sides of two maturing-vats reared up like black sails.

I forced myself to act. For fifteen minutes, taut with apprehension, I conducted a search, examining every spare yard of the place and even, on occasions, looking under flat-topped boulders. I knew what I expected to find. But in the end I found nothing.

Relief surged in like a tide – relief and thankfulness. I persuaded myself that the screams I'd heard had been imaginary, like the flashing lights. For most of those lost eight hours I'd probably lain peacefully asleep amongst the bracken.

My next business was to find the particular part of the wall into which my cigarette-case had dropped. Details came back to me. I'd stumbled against the wall and steadied myself against hollow-sounding metal. The place I was looking for, therefore, must be at the north-east corner, where the remains of one of the vats stood close against the wall.

I began to search there, pulling out stones and thrusting my arm into nooks and crannies; but almost at once my eye caught a movement in the faraway fields above the village and the hotel.

I straightened up and watched. About a score of men, like a line of beaters on a grouse-moor, were moving up in my direction. A few carried shot-guns.

It took me several moments to realize what was happening. At first I had the frightening idea that they might be looking for me; but then I remembered about the escaped murderer, and their purpose became plain. Willie Ross's words echoed in my head: 'When the fog lifts they'll soon find him. He can't escape from Kersivay.'

At such a distance it was impossible to recognize individuals; but I supposed that the party would include police, warders and medical attendants from the prison and local men who were able to afford a day off work.

I could not now return directly to the hotel without meeting them, and I didn't want to meet them. Nor did I want to be discovered in this area of the ruined factory. I made no attempt to analyse my reasons.

I abandoned the search for my cigarette-case and

set off in a south-easterly direction, taking care to keep out of sight by following the old grass-grown track from the factory. Leading down through a narrow glen, this track, I remembered, met the main road only a few hundred yards from the Big House. It seemed to me that on the main road I should be outside the search party's operational focus. In any case, I could bear to meet people on a public thoroughfare. I had every right to be there.

Birds sang amongst the brambles on either side. Hazel trees gave off the earthy scent of autumn. After a time the glen widened out into farmland; but on my left a high ridge remained between me and the beaters.

I found that I was hungry and dying for a smoke. In spite of this, however, I was in reasonably good spirits.

The evil mood of the night before had been sloughed aside. I had tholed another black-out, this time apparently without any of the dire consequences I had feared; and I was beginning to hope that its cause was simply a violent migraine brought on by my overwork and obsessive memories of Myra. When I had breakfasted and changed my clothes I should be a new man, ready to bring my tape-recorder into action. With the news of a murderer's escape adding spice to local comment, the programme suggested by the Laughing Cavalier might now prove to be a real winner.

There was a chance, too, that my absence from the hotel might not have been noticed. I had left the bar soon after the news about Terry Jackson was brought in by the schoolmaster; and in their excitement Willie Ross, Nappy Neil and the others could easily have overlooked my sudden disappearance. If they thought about it at all they'd probably decide that I'd gone outside to attend to the wants of nature and had retired later, via the hotel front door, to my bedroom.

The track crossed empty stubble-fields, subsequently skirting a strip of woodland. The village came into view again, miles away on the low ground by the sea, and I saw breakfast smoke beginning to rise from its chimneys. Behind the trees to my right a collie was barking, and through the tall trunks I glimpsed Ayrshire cattle being gathered in for milking. A young man in overalls appeared at a gate and shouted to the dog, but he didn't see me.

As the track began to climb again, cultivated ground gave place to moorland. Black-faced sheep pattered out of my way, then turned to stare with stupid eyes.

Presently the Big House was less than half-a-mile away, its garden blazing with dahlias and roses – just as I had remembered it. I wondered if Roderick Dhu still tended the flowers. Surprisingly, I had no feeling of nostalgia in the presence of my old home. Perhaps it represented too many sad memories – memories especially of my father's pain.

The track ran parallel with its boundary wall, not far from the main entrance. As I reached a point opposite the front gate a broad man in plus-fours came striding down the drive. He had a military air, even to the way he carried a gun sloped on his left shoulder.

He saw me, and his momentary pause showed that my sudden appearance had startled him.

I climbed a fence and met him on the main road

outside his gate. Blue eyes, sharp and questioning, studied my face and the rumpled state of my clothes.

'Good morning. You must be Major Rivington-Keel?' I said.

'Afraid you have me at a disadvantage.'

His grey moustache only partially concealed the scar on his upper lip. A hard slurring in his speech indicated that the wound also affected the inside of his mouth. Professionally, this disappointed me. He wasn't a good radio prospect.

I told him who I was and the purpose of my visit to the island.

His cagey expression changed. 'Thought you were the damned murderer!' He smiled, crookedly, and I guessed his age to be about sixty. 'Prison rang me up last night. Warning, you know. Said they'd be organizing a search-party when the fog cleared in the morning. Decided to look around on my own before breakfast.'

'Don't you know what Jackson looks like?'

'Never set eyes on him. Chap who phoned didn't enlighten me much, either. Said he's young, about five foot six – that was all. Can see now you're a bit taller.'

'They're beating up from the village now,' I said.

'Which way?'

'Towards Hirsay. I imagine they'll sweep round into *Gleann nan Taibhis*.'

He nodded. 'Damned awkward! If – if anything were to happen, I mean. Hope they find him.'

'I can't see he's got much chance. Kersivay's not all that big. Somebody's bound to spot him.'

'Poor devil!' He frowned and lowered the gun,

cradling it in the crook of his arm. 'The mental agony those men must suffer!'

'I know,' I said.

There was a little pause.

'Had breakfast?' he inquired, abruptly.

'Not yet. I developed a headache – couldn't sleep – so I got up early for some fresh air.'

'Feeling better?'

'Yes, indeed. I walked round by the Hirsay Cliff and back along the old track from the factory.'

'Weren't you afraid you'd meet the murderer?'

'That didn't occur to me.'

'I see.' Suddenly the coldness drained from his eyes. 'Well,' he mumbled, affably, 'what about it? Breakfast, I mean – see your old home again.'

'I'd have to ring the hotel and let them know.'

'I'll do that. Give you an alibi!'

'Well, thank you very much. I could be doing with a spot of breakfast. And a smoke. I forgot to bring cigarettes.'

'Fine!' He put his free arm about my shoulders. 'Come along, Mr Parsons. Englishman myself. Try to keep the Highland tradition going, though. Open house.'

I told him I'd never seen any difference between English and Highland hospitality. He seemed surprised.

As we approached the front door I said: 'Who looks after the garden?'

'Didn't you know? Roderick McLeod and his wife stayed on.' He pointed to a smartly painted building separated by a courtyard from the main part of the house. 'I converted the old stables. They live there now – not in the house as in your time. They like a bit of privacy in the evenings. So do I.'

He racked his gun in a side-room off the hall. At one time it had been my father's study. From the kitchen premises came the smell of frying bacon.

'Like a wash?' he said, glancing at my hands. 'While I telephone the hotel.'

'Please. I had a fall amongst the bracken on the Hirsay Cliff.'

'Thought so. Know your way?'

'Yes, thanks.'

The stone stairs were carpeted now, the bathroom fittings of chrome instead of brass. There was hot water, too, even at half past seven in the morning. Our old range had obviously been superseded by an electric cooker and immerser.

When I came down, feeling hungrier than ever, Maggie McLeod was waiting in the hall. The fair hair I remembered was now white, the bloom on her plump cheeks faded and almost gone.

'The Major told me. Oh, Master Peter!'

I kissed her. 'Maggie, it's wonderful to see you! How's Roderick?'

'He is well. Still grumbling away.' She smiled. 'But och, what a time to be calling on us! You haven't changed, *laochain* – always doing the unexpected!'

She went on talking but made no mention of my mother.

We were moving towards the dining-room when a cavernous cough came from the kitchen-passage. Out of the shadows appeared Roderick Dhu, glum as an undertaker, his thin face oddly white in contrast with his black hair. It was the face for a high stiff collar and a frock coat. Instead he was in shirt-sleeves and wore brown corduroy trousers.

'Good old Roderick!' I exclaimed. 'I was sure you were still at the Big House when I saw the dahlias!'

He shook his head. 'You are looking old for your years!' he announced, sadly.

'Och, for goodness sake – you don't look so young yourself!' Maggie put an edge on her soft voice. 'Can't you give Master Peter a better welcome than that?'

'I am not sure if Kersivay has a welcome for anybody nowadays.' Then for a moment he indulged in the ghost of a smile. 'But I am glad you have come, Mr Parsons. You were a throughither boy, but kind. And I had a great respect for your father.'

He turned suddenly and shuffled off, back into the shadows.

'You see – he hasn't changed!' Maggie shrugged. 'It's the Free Kirk upbringing he had. But he's a good man and a good husband all the same!'

Major Rivington-Keel was waiting for me in the dining-room.

'Spoke to Rona Carmichael on the phone,' he said. 'She wasn't long up. Didn't seem to know you were out.'

This was a relief. There was a good chance now that nobody would ever realize I hadn't slept the night in my room. The chamber-maid would even find that my bed-clothes were disturbed, for during the afternoon, in the course of trying to cure my headache, I had partially undressed and crawled in beneath the quilt.

Maggie served us with bacon and eggs from the sideboard, then retired to attend the wants of her husband in the kitchen.

I enjoyed my breakfast and the cigarette which followed it. We exchanged talk about the house and the estate, and I had the impression that the Major was a much more efficient laird than my father had been. Probably because of his military background. He'd been born of a family of soldiers in Sussex.

'Not many of the Rivington-Keels left now,' he told me. 'Got a distant cousin in Canada. Last of the line, he and I.'

He'd been drafted into a Scottish battalion in the final years of the war – the old Royal Scots Fusiliers. 'Fine bunch of chaps. Persuaded me Scotland was the best place to retire to – especially the islands.'

One thing was certain: he had a great deal of money. The lavish way he'd decorated and furnished the Big House – even his own well-cut tweeds – provided evidence of that.

He went on: 'Mind you, didn't mean to retire so soon. But I got my packet – bullet in the mouth – less than a week before the Germans packed in. Outside Lübeck. Nazis took me prisoner, bunged me into a concentration camp hospital near Berlin, where the Yanks found me. Spent six months in England getting over it, then heard this estate was on the market.'

'You've never regretted buying it?'

'Well, must be frank. Lonely sometimes. Difficult to make friends with the islanders.'

I nodded. 'Anybody whose family hasn't lived in Kersivay for at least two hundred years is an "incomer"!'

'However,' he continued, reaching for the marmalade. 'I like the peace of it– and I like farming. And when I get fed-up I beat it. Paris, Monte Carlo, sometimes a little town called Haaltert in Belgium. Joined the R.S.F. in Haaltert – February '45, just before we got cracking on the final push.' He paused for a moment, a curious glint in his eye. 'Old bachelor,' he grinned, suddenly. 'But have my moments.'

He took out his pipe. I lit a second cigarette. We were discussing the radio documentary I had in mind, and he was suggesting a few possible contacts amongst the prison staff, when the telephone rang in the hall outside. A minute later Maggie came in, her face pinched and anxious.

'Major, that was Joanna's mother – ringing up from the kiosk in the village. Joanna didn't get home last night.'

'What!' His stubbly red face grew redder still, the colour rising into a broad bald patch above his forehead. 'You told me she left your place at seven o'clock!'

'So she did, sir. Roderick and I were wanting her to stay the night, on account of the fog. But you know Joanna – so pert and sure of herself. "I've been out in a fog before. Besides, my boy friend's waiting for me". Though who her boy friend is I wouldn't be knowing. And Joanna certainly wouldn't be telling!'

The Major glanced at me. 'Joanna Campbell. A girl I engaged about six months ago to help Mrs MacLeod with the housework. Comes in the morning – on her bicycle – and generally goes home at night.'

'A cousin of wee Katie McCuish, the waitress at the hotel,' explained Maggie, quietly. 'Lives with her widowed mother next door to the shop. Prettier than Katie, but a different sort of girl altogether.'

Nobody mentioned Terry Jackson, the man on the run. I thought back. It had been about half past eight when the schoolmaster brought into the bar the news of his escape. When she left the Big House at seven, therefore, Joanna Campbell couldn't have known that she faced a more dangerous hazard than the fog.

'What are we to do, sir? Mrs Campbell wasn't really worried at all, thinking that Roderick and I had kept Joanna with us, as we often do in bad weather. She rang up just to make sure she was all right. Now she's in a terrible state!'

'Don't blame her.' The Major got up, frowning over his pipe. 'All the same, couldn't the girl simply be having a night out with this boy friend of hers?'

'It wouldn't be the first time!' Maggie was still cattish, despite her anxiety. 'That's why I'm not so keen on going to the police. Think of all the scandal it might stir up!' She pursed her lips, then slowly relented. 'But after all she is a human being – a good girl at her work, if at nothing else. I mean, if anything *has* happened to her—'

The bell rang at the front door. Maggie started and hurried out.

She came back with Kenneth Harringay. He wore an ancient brown tweed suit, and the hat with the flies in it was in his hand.

He seemed astonished to find me there. After a moment's hesitation he nodded in my direction, then turned to the Major.

'I was out with the search-party,' he said. 'I am sorry to have to tell you that we've just found Joanna Campbell's body. Dead. On the shore under Hirsay Cliff.'

4

The Evil of Arrogance

TERRY JACKSON had done it. Everybody would say that Terry Jackson had done it. Time and again I told myself savagely that Terry Jackson *must* have done it.

Those screams. I'd heard them while fully aware of my surroundings. Not later. They were no subconscious memory – of that I was sure.

Of that I was almost sure.

There were only three policemen on Kersivay – Sergeant McPhee, Constable McKechnie and Constable Anderson. The first two had gone with the search-party. Constable Anderson had remained at the police station in the village, not only to keep an eye on routine affairs but also in case news of Terry Jackson might arrive from an unexpected quarter.

Now Sergeant McPhee was guarding the body on the shore, while Harringay phoned Dr Barbour from the Big House, suggesting he should come and make a preliminary examination on the spot.

To keep the numbers of the search-party up to strength, the Major and I decided to join it. The optimism of the past hour had left me, and I felt the need of action as an antidote to unpleasant thoughts.

Harringay guided us to where the beaters continued to operate amongst the sand-dunes, south-east of the prison. Already they had moved more than a mile from where Joanna Campbell's body had been found.

For two hours we trudged in open order round the broad shoulders of Hirsay. Then we made a wide circle behind the Big House and descended into *Gleann nan Taibhis,* where the breeze no longer cooled us. We ploughed through briar clumps and hazel trees on either side of the burn – sweating, thorns tearing at our clothes, footgear caked with gluey mud.

When we reached a point about a third of the way down the glen – with a waterfall making heavy music to our left – someone on the right of the line raised an alarm. We moved quickly to the opposite side of the glen and surrounded a wide area of whins. But when Constable McKechnie and two of the warders went through it, parting the prickly, tough branches with their sticks, the alarm proved to have been false.

We resumed the open-order search, but in the next hour we flushed nothing except protesting birds and a few startled rabbits.

During part of this time I had as my closest companion a medical orderly from the prison – a tough Glaswegian, whose name was Alec Thomson. At one time he had played professional football for Rangers.

He was shocked by the escape of Terry Jackson and its tragic consequence. 'It's no' bloody possible!' he exclaimed, as we squelched through soapy marshland at the bottom of the glen. 'It's no' bloody possible – but it happened!'

At one point I said: 'Are the security arrangements not pretty thorough?'

'You're tellin' me they're thorough! The boss was

keen for to make a go of it – I mean, after all the bloody song an' dance there was when the place was built. Roll-call three times a day, prisoners never allowed outside the grounds in any circumstances. But the main thing, Mr Parsons – the main thing is, yon wall is just no' climbable!'

'Then how did Jackson do it?'

'I can maybe see how his absence wasn't noticed. He was all right, you know – except just sometimes when he took a headache and went crazy crackers for a while. But we always had plenty o' warnin' if an attack was comin' on, and then we'd shoot him full o' dope and plunk him in bed. There's a lot o' them like that. But normally he was as sensible an' reliable as you and me. Keen on the garden – used to spend bloody hours on the rose-beds. The warders never bothered. On a good day they'd park him in the garden after lunch and leave him to his own devices. There's only one way in and out, you see – a gate leading to the courtyard at the back. And somebody's always on duty there. When the fog came down it didn't make any difference. There was still only one way out.'

'He found another, though.'

'Ay. He climbed the wall. And if you ask me, Mr Parsons, he had help from outside! Yon wall is no' climbable, I'm tellin' you! Twenty feet high and smooth as a baby's backside. He must have had the end of a rope thrown over to him.'

'Was he friendly with any of the islanders?'

'Not to my knowledge. Plenty folk in and out, of course – pals o' the high heid yins. The minister and the priest, the polis, Dr Barbour, Major Rivington-Keen, Mr Ross from the hotel – and strangers whiles, like Mr Harringay. Yon's him with Major Rivington-Keel and Constable McKechnie at the far end o' the line.'

'I know,' I said.

He frowned. 'Why should any o' that lot help a prisoner to escape?'

It was an unanswerable question. In any case I was thinking of something else.

'You said you could always tell when Jackson was going to have one of his attacks?'

'Ay. This time it must have come on him quick. He was perfectly normal yesterday. In fact, after the escape was reported, the boss told us he didn't reckon anything very terrible would happen. Not for a day or two, anyway. And by then he hoped Jackson would be back inside.'

'But something terrible did happen!'

'That's the damned thing, Mr Parsons! That's the damned peculiar thing!'

We crossed a fence on to the main road, where the other members of the party were collecting, and I had no further opportunity of talking to him.

Shortly after midday we straggled into the village. At the police station we reported failure.

By now Sergeant McPhee had been released from his duty of guarding the body. It had been brought in by a tractor and trailer requisitioned from a farmer, he told us, and, following a post mortem examination by Dr Barbour in his surgery, had been handed over to Mrs Campbell and her relatives. He had arranged to lead another search-party in the afternoon, he said, over in the direction of Unival.

Finally he dismissed us – to eat and rest if we could.

The sorrow in the grey crooked streets of the village was almost a tangible thing. So was the mounting fear.

Murdo Cameron had closed the school, and the children were being kept indoors; but a small crowd of men and women gathered round us for news. Though their voices were quiet, the lilting Gaelic vowels had taken on a flat quality of acute uneasiness.

I was uneasy, too.

Members of the prison staff went off in a car which had been specially sent for them. Men from the village disappeared into their own houses. Major Rivington-Keel had hired a car from the small garage next door to the police station and now offered to take Harringay and me back to the hotel, before returning home himself.

Harringay accepted the invitation; but I declined.

'Someone to see in the village. I'll be in for lunch, though,' I told Harringay.

He glanced at my face. 'Sure you're all right?' he inquired.

'Quite sure.'

The Major smiled his crooked smile. 'City type. Tiring, all this exercise. All the same, should do you good, Parsons. See you again, I hope. In more pleasant circumstances.'

They drove away.

The hotel station-wagon was parked outside the smaller of the two shops and I had an idea that Nappy Neil might be inside, collecting groceries and talking to his future in-laws. I was assured of a lift back to the hotel, and in any case I needed cigarettes. Principally, however, I wanted to see old Annie Mary McCuish. Not only was she grandmother to wee Katie, Nappy Neil's intended; she was grandmother also to

Joanna Campbell. I felt I ought to offer her my sympathy.

Crossing the street, I entered the shop to the tinkle of a bell. After the sharp morning air the aroma of mixed groceries was heavily sweet. Behind the main counter stood shelves piled with bottles, tins and packets. On the left a smart showcase displayed cigarettes and paperbacks; on the right a more austere side-counter supported large bottles filled with the famous treacle-toffee.

From the back premises came a fresh woman of middle age whom I recognized as wee Katie's mother – Arabella McCuish, whose husband, Annie Mary's son, had been lost during the war in an Arctic convoy. Her eyes were red, and at first she looked at me without expression. But when I told her who I was, she greeted me with a slightly emotional warmth.

'Come away ben, Mister Peter. The old lady would like to see you.'

'I'd like to see her, too.'

'Nappy Neil is in. He has just been telling us about you.'

I asked for a packet of cigarettes; and as she tore off its wrapping, counted out my change and then conducted me down a dark passage to the kitchen, she continued to talk – about the tragic death of poor Joanna, about the threat which now hung over the whole island, about the fog which had kept both Katie and Nappy Neil at the hotel the night before.

'But they phoned us, and we knew they would be all right. We locked ourselves in, Annie Mary and I – safe and snug – never dreaming of the terrible sadness that would be coming to her next door.'

The kitchen was delicately scented with peat-smoke. Leaning carelessly against an old-fashioned dresser, Nappy Neil offered me a smile as I came in, but it looked unnatural. By the glowing range sat Annie Mary, muffled in shawls, her hair a fragile silver halo. When her daughter-in-law introduced me, she put her stick aside, pulled me down with knuckly, twisted hands and kissed me.

'Such a time to be coming back, *loachain*!' Her voice was frail, though I noticed that at times her dark brown eyes were as keen as ever. 'A sad, sad day it is, for Kersivay!'

Haltingly I said how sorry I was about what had happened.

She nodded. 'Joanna has gone to her rest. May it be peaceful. More peaceful than her life in this world.'

I caught Nappy Neil's eye. He shrugged. Through the wall someone was weeping. Mrs Campbell probably, contemplating a coffin and the shrouded remains of Joanna.

The bell rang in the shop, and Katie's mother left us. I sat down on a wooden stool by the old lady's chair. She held my hand, murmuring to herself in Gaelic.

Then her bearing became more alert. 'I mind when you were only a laddie,' she said.

'You used to give Nappy Neil and me toffee.'

'Ay, many a time.' She smiled, eyes sparkling. 'A throughither pair you were – especially Nappy Neil. Little did I think when he was stealing my apples that one day he would be after my grand-daughter!'

Nappy Neil grinned. 'It's a slander! I never stole your apples in my life, Annie Mary!'

'No, I was too clever and too quick for you. But you were *wanting* to steal my apples!'

'Something in that, maybe!'

Her expression changed. She was like many old people, her thoughts often sliding out of focus.

'If only Joanna had been a nice quiet girl like Katie! But she was wild, wild. Philandering with men and boasting about it, and caring nothing for the disgrace to her people.'

'I used to wonder about those men,' said Nappy Neil, shifting uncomfortably against the dresser. 'Who were they, Annie Mary? We never found out.'

She ignored him. 'It was the father she had – Alistair Campbell, who came across from the mainland to work at the fishing. A fine looking man with a lust for life – and a lust for women, too. But my daughter would have him, come what might.'

'He died like a hero, anyway,' said Nappy Neil.

'Ay. That awful day! Nobody but Alistair would have gone down the cliff. He rescued a wee boy, Peter – a visitor's laddie who had no knowledge of the tides – but he himself fell to his death, near where Joanna fell. They will be saying it is more than a coincidence. They will be saying it is a judgement.'

The kitchen was hot with the fire and the sunlight. Katie's mother was still in the shop, talking to a customer. I should have been congratulating myself on having found a wonderful personality for my tape-recorder; but for all I cared at that moment, tape-recorders might never have existed.

Annie Mary's mood remained sombre. Her fingers were hard in my hand, like the links of a chain.

'You will be seeing a difference in Kersivay?' she said.

'Quite a difference,' I agreed. 'There's the electricity, the air service – and now the prison—'

'I did not mean it in that way. Are you not seeing a difference among the people?'

'They seem more prosperous, more up to date,' I began; but again she interrupted.

'*Laochain,* you have not been here long enough to know. But you will know quite soon. Evil has come to Kersivay.'

'You mean the prison? Murderers who can escape—'

'No, no! That we can understand. The evil I speak of is hard to understand.'

I could feel her hand trembling. Her eyes filmed over; her voice had grown shrill. I glanced up at Nappy Neil.

He shook his head. 'She's always laying off like this. We can't make head or tail of it.'

Annie Mary stared into the red heart of the range. 'It is the evil of arrogance,' she said, whispering now. 'The evil that thinks nothing of killing in order to preserve itself, that looks upon all life as unimportant except its own. But, *laochain,* a day is coming – and coming soon – when evil will no longer triumph, and sweetness of spirit will return to Kersivay.'

For a moment she had me under a spell. For a moment I could sense evil swirling round us like a fog. Then her daughter-in-law returned from the shop, and revelation was cut off as if by a closing curtain.

'What has she been saying?' Arabella looked across at Nappy Neil.

'Ach, it's the mood on her again.' He stood up and stretched, attempting perhaps to shake off unpleasant thoughts. 'Peter and I will have to be going if he's to be in time for lunch.'

I shook hands with the old lady, but her thoughts

were elsewhere. We left her whispering Gaelic to some unseen audience.

Arabella saw us to the shop door. As she waved us off, she was dabbing at her eyes with a handkerchief.

The road was deserted. I doubted if many would use it for walking until Terry Jackson had been caught. During the morning I had seen some farmers working at the harvest, stacking corn. Now there was no movement in the fields, no bustle of life. Kersivay was mourning for Joanna.

'It was the way she dressed,' said Nappy Neil, driving fast towards the hotel. 'Very smart – sexy a bit. Didn't suit the older folk.' Obliquely he was apologizing for Annie Mary's diatribe. 'There was one thing, though, nobody knew where she got the money for her fal-de-rals. When Katie would ask her about it, she'd just laugh and say she charged high prices – making out she was a whore.'

'According to Maggie MacLeod she left the Big House at seven o'clock last night to meet someone. Someone she called her boy friend. The fog didn't worry her.'

Nappy Neil swung the station-wagon into the hotel yard, jerking it to a halt. He was usually a more competent driver.

'And met Terry Jackson instead,' he muttered.

'Looks like it.'

'I hope to God they catch him soon!'

After a wash and a change I went to the dining-room and found Harringay finishing his soup. He seemed glad that I should sit at the same small table.

Today no one had thought of taking a picnic basket to the shore or to the moor, and in consequence the place was fairly full. Three waitresses were on duty;

but Katie wasn't one of them. Sorrowing for her cousin, she probably preferred to wash dishes in the scullery rather than face the guests.

Harringay saw me picking at my food. 'A bit under the weather?' he inquired.

'I'm not used to all this excitement.'

'You must have gone early to bed last night.' He appeared to be engrossed in dissecting the cold wing of a chicken. 'I came in about half past nine, expecting to find you in the lounge, but you'd disappeared.'

'I had a headache. It was still there at six o'clock this morning. The fog had lifted, so I decided to go for a walk. I went round by the old sea-weed factory and was eventually captured by the Major.'

'Pity about the headache.' He had a habit of studying one's face and then looking down again with hooded eyes, and I had a feeling that my laborious explanation had only made him more suspicious. Quietly he added: 'Did you know Terry Jackson was on the run?'

'Yes. The schoolmaster came in to tell us last night. But I'm afraid I was so miserable I forgot all about him.'

'Odd,' he commented, helping himself to more salad.

There was a brittle silence. Kenneth Harringay ought to have been gentle, even bumbling, for these were the natural attributes of a fisherman-poet. Instead, he sounded like a detective.

I made up my mind to counter-attack. 'I was looking for you last night. It astonished me you should have risked going out in that fog.'

He smiled as he asked the waitress to bring him biscuits and cheese. 'I didn't go far. Just down the road to the village. I wanted to have a word with Joanna Campbell.'

Excitement stirred, as if I were teetering on the verge of a discovery. 'But – but she didn't go home last night.'

'That's why I came back here at half past nine. Her mother was convinced she wouldn't be coming – on account of the fog.'

For a second or two I allowed the conversation to rest there, in case he might volunteer more information. But he said nothing. I was fascinated by his strong, brown hands as they broke a water-biscuit in half.

Finally I put the question that troubled me. 'Did you know Joanna Campbell?'

'Not personally. Only by repute.' A bleakness came into his voice. 'But like Victor Hugo we must have pity on the dead.'

As we finished our meal he said: 'By the way, I have something to show you. Let's have our coffee in the billiards-room. It's usually pretty quiet there after lunch.'

We went through the busy lounge and along the passage beyond it. A small tension pain nagged at the pit of my stomach.

The billiards-room was empty. Situated at the back of the hotel, its windows looked out on flat scrub-land to the north. They caught no sunlight, and in consequence the place was cold. The green baize table, the cue-racks and marker-boards, the worn grey linoleum – all had a tawdry air.

A waitress followed us in, carrying coffee and cups on a pewter tray. When she left us I began to pour out.

'Sugar?' I said.

'Two spoonfuls, please.' Harringay put his hand in his pocket and took out a silver cigarette-case. 'This yours?' he inquired.

I recognized it at once.

5

Rona

It had been a present from Myra, in the early days. On its face a scroll-work design enclosed my initials in the centre.

'It's mine,' I said, flatly. 'Where did you find it?'

Eyelids lowered, Harringay balanced it in his hand. 'Near the wall of the old factory. When we found Joanna Campbell's body they sent me to the Big House to phone for Dr Barbour. But of course you know that. As I was passing the factory I saw a glint of metal under the wall. The sun was low at the time and shining directly into the crevice, otherwise I don't suppose I'd have spotted it.'

'Why didn't you mention it this morning?'

'I didn't connect it with you – not until later, when I had a closer look and saw the initials. Indeed, what with all the excitement, I forgot about it until just before lunch. I meant to hand it over to the police. Perhaps it's just as well I didn't.'

'I missed it when I got to the Big House. Couldn't think where I dropped it. But of course I did come round by the factory. I told you.'

'Yes, you told me.'

He opened the case. Inside were half a dozen cigarettes, damp and disintegrating.

He said: 'One thing puzzles me, though. Why are the cigarettes so wet?'

'How d'you mean?'

'You say you dropped the case this morning, after the fog cleared and the rain went off. It had sprung open certainly – probably as it hit the ground. Nevertheless, the cigarettes inside ought to have been bone dry. As it was – well, my first impression was that it had been lying there all night.'

'The grass was soaking,' I reminded him.

'It was lying on top of a boulder.' The hood came off his eyes and for a time we stared at each other. Then, unexpectedly, he smiled and shrugged. 'One of life's little mysteries,' he said, snapping the case shut. 'Though between ourselves, I'm like Scott – "I love not mystery or doubt".'

I feel sure he intended to return my property. Before he could do so, however, voices approached in the passage, and – perhaps absent-mindedly – he slipped the case into his own pocket. I had no further opportunity to ask him for it.

The door opened. On the threshold stood the King of Kersivay, accompanied by Murdo Cameron and a youngish man with a toothbrush moustache whom I didn't know. They seemed surprised to see us. Even taken aback.

But the schoolmaster soon recovered. 'Man, man!' he exclaimed. 'There you are at last, Peter! They told me you were here, but of course so much has been happening we didn't have a chance to meet. How are you, boy?'

He exuded turbulence like a north-west wind. A daunting performance until you came to understand that its purpose was to camouflage shyness and to compensate in some degree for his failure to right all the wrongs in this world.

The King interrupted our high-powered exchange of news. 'I don't think you've met Dr Barbour, Peter.' The shirt-sleeved camaraderie of last night in the bar had given place to a more sophisticated mood, redolent of Kirk plates, solid bank balances and County Councils. He was acting mine host now, wearing an enormous checked tweed suit and trying to soften the hoarse cadences of his voice as he carried out a social duty. 'Mr Peter Parsons, the wireless producer. Dr James Barbour.'

The doctor was smart. That was evident at once. Later on I discovered that he was also extremely good at his job. But I didn't take to him much. His smile was facile, his handshake perfunctory, and I had the feeling that his cold blue eyes were already probing my malaise.

'An old inhabitant?' he said.

'As old as the hills!' declared Murdo Cameron. 'His folks, I mean. The Parsons and the Rosses came to Kersivay in the sixteenth century – after being thrown out of Ireland for sheep-stealing!'

The King's hard, dour face broke into a sunny smile. 'Then we lived a quiet life until Murdo arrived to shake us up!'

Harringay, it seemed, knew both the schoolmaster and the doctor quite well. As we talked, I gathered that during the summer, with Major Rivington-Keel often making up a foursome, they had shot and fished together. But I found it difficult to concentrate. The matter of the cigarette-case was an irritating burr in my mind.

It soon became apparent, however, that the three

men had come to the billiards-room to do more than enjoy light conversation, though I believe they welcomed it as a temporary anodyne for anxiety.

The King rang for a waitress and ordered five Drambuies. The atmosphere changed. Again I was conscious of the drabness and coldness of the room.

Harringay said: 'If you wish to talk privately, Mr Parsons and I were just leaving.'

The King reassured him. 'There's nothing private. It's something that concerns us all.'

'Too damned true it does!' growled the schoolmaster. 'The position's this. Sergeant McPhee has been wondering if he ought to ask for help from the C.I.D. I gave him my opinion, and he asked me to get Mr Ross's. Actually, I think the C.I.D. should be brought in. Mr Ross doesn't.'

'Not yet, anyway.' The King spoke without heat. 'They're bound to catch up with Terry Jackson by this evening. Then the sad affair may settle down.'

'Settle down my foot! Man, can't you face up to it? There's a whole tribe of reporters coming with the afternoon plane. They telephoned for rooms at Mrs McIntosh's boarding-house in the village. She told me so herself. This thing won't settle down, no matter what happens. And why should it? That prison ought never to have been built in the first place, and I'll do my damnedest to have it removed even yet!' In a changed voice he added: 'Joanna Campbell may not have died in vain after all. Poor Joanna. She was kind, in her own fashion.'

The drinks came in. We sat down on the tatty chairs at the far end of the table.

'Good for you, Murdo!' said the King, calmly. 'However, before we get in too much of a panic, let's hear what the doctor has to say.'

Somewhat smugly, Dr Barbour knuckled one side of his stubby moustache: 'Sergeant McPhee suggested I should let you know the result of my post mortem. Unexpected features,' he said, in the genteel accent of Edinburgh University.

'How d'you mean – unexpected features?' demanded the schoolmaster.

'Well, Joanna Campbell died soon after midnight. She was killed by a blow on the back of the head with some kind of blunt instrument – a cosh, the branch of a tree, even a shinty-stick – it's difficult to tell. Then, some time after death, the body was thrown over the cliff. There was no evidence of sexual assault.'

The King's face took on a hard inscrutability. I found myself gulping the Drambuie, and that may have been the cause of a choking sensation in my throat.

'What's unexpected about all that?' I said.

Murdo Cameron threw himself back in his chair gesturing approval. 'Right, Peter! Come on, James – what's unexpected about all that? And don't start giving us a lot of your psychiatric clap-trap!'

But Harringay put in, quietly: 'I see what he means. Not a typical case of murder by a psychopath?'

'Exactly.' Dr Barbour was smooth. 'Terry Jackson's previous victim was killed in a frenzy of perverted lust while the fit was on him. One would have expected a similar pattern in this case.'

'Ach, you're trying to be too clever!' the schoolmaster threw at him. 'Terry Jackson's a killer and ought to have been hanged. This black-out lark, it's only an excuse.'

'I don't agree, Murdo.'

'Nobody's asking you to agree! But I'm telling you, boy – the evil that's in a man comes out. If Terry Jackson could kill once in one way, he can kill again in another. You back me up, there, don't you, Peter?'

I had to struggle to make sounds of agreement. But in fact nobody was interested in my reactions – not at that particular time.

Creasing his brows, the King said: 'What are you getting at, Doctor?'

'I'm not sure.' He crossed his legs, hitching up his trousers with almost feminine care. 'Incidentally,' he continued, 'there's something else you ought to know. The prison people – and Sergeant McPhee – they're all convinced that Terry Jackson had outside assistance in making his escape. Not only that. It appears that during yesterday morning he showed no symptoms at all of impending psychosis.'

The King said nothing, but a small sad smile appeared on Kenneth Harringay's face. Blood pistoned through the veins in my head.

It was the schoolmaster who broke the silence. 'Well, my God, if this is true, then the C.I.D. must certainly be brought in!'

'You're right, Murdo.' The King's admission came with reluctance. 'I was hoping to save something from the wreck of Kersivay's reputation. Now it seems we're in for it in any case.'

Suddenly gentle, Murdo Cameron patted his arm. 'A surgical operation, Willie. Unpleasant, but the only cure.' He paused for a second, then added with renewed venom: 'There's something rotten in Kersivay. I've known it for a long time.'

The King jerked his head up. In profile it had a leonine power and challenge.

'What the hell d'you mean by that?'

'You know fine what I mean. We've talked about it before. I realize you don't like it, Willie, because you're the boss and Kersivay is your life, and you can't bear to admit its character has changed. Look! When I came here at first, before the war, people had some regard for the things of the spirit. I don't mean they were a lot of dreary psalm-singers, but they had some respect for kirk and chapel. They could make whoopee at a ceilidh but still have time to possess their souls and be gentle with their neighbours. In other words, their sense of values was reasonably adjusted. Now they're after the main chance – most of them at any rate. No time for religious discipline. No time for the sweeter acts of living. Money spells influence and success. Their aim is materialism – like it was in Hitler's Germany.'

The King seemed to sag a little in his chair, an old lion troubled by a yelping jackal. But the doctor only smiled with the superiority of a scientist discounting ill-informed criticism from a layman.

Kenneth Harringay's reaction was different. He sat forward, quietly alert.

'Tell me, Murdo. This – this rottenness you refer to – do you mean it existed in Kersivay even before the prison was built?'

'Ay. It was there, under the surface. But the prison was the first ugly flower to blossom on the weed. Now the crop is multiplying.'

Dr Barbour finished his drink. 'Surely the charge of materialism can be brought against a good many places besides Kersivay? I think you're being a bit fanciful, Murdo!'

'Fanciful? Don't you believe it! And here's another thing. You and your kind are playing the devil's game. You find psychological excuses for every kind of evil. But a sin's a sin, James, no matter how it's tarted up. Take the commandments. "Thou shalt not commit adultery." It doesn't add, "except in certain circumstances outlined by Freud". "Thou shalt not kill." It doesn't add, "except when thou hast a black-out – caused by resentment at thy mother's whoredom – in which case all will be forgiven".'

My nerves were twanging. I twisted the liqueur glass in my hands until its contents came perilously near to being spilt. I found Kenneth Harringay looking in my direction and strove to be still.

Dr Barbour laughed. 'What a lot of nonsense you do talk, Murdo—'

'That's enough!' The King cut him short, slapping the arm of his chair. 'Murdo – go back to the police station. Tell Sergeant McPhee we'll have no objection even if every detective on the mainland is brought in. But for God's sake tell him, too, that we want this murderer caught—'

There was a brief knocking. The door opened.

Rona Carmichael came in, tall, trim and fresh. 'The telephone, Mr Parsons, please. A call from London.'

I got up, quickly. Leaving the room in her wake, I heard the others moving, too. Dr Barbour was offering to drive the schoolmaster back to the village. Harringay was telling the King he intended to go out and probably wouldn't be in again until the small hours of the morning, and I heard him mention my name. Then he said something about paying another visit to Joanna Campbell's home.

Suddenly an alliterative phrase ran dancing into my head. Harringay and the harlot. Harringay and the harlot. The partners whirled. I wondered how and where they had been introduced.

We came to the front hall.

Rona Carmichael said: 'This box, Mr Parsons.'

As I had expected, my caller was the Laughing Cavalier. 'Well, Peter, according to the early editions of the evening papers, you've got yourself a real scoop this time!'

'It's pretty grim,' I told him.

'Yes, I can believe that. Getting some good interviews?'

'Not yet. Look, for the moment the programme we visualized has gone for a burton. Some people would talk too much, others not at all. Difficult to find a balance. In any case, at this stage we're all looking askance at one another. You know what it's like in a small, self-contained community. Meantime I'd say it's a matter for the News Department.'

His sigh was audible along four hundred miles of wire. 'I suppose you're right,' he agreed, reluctantly.

'But afterwards,' I said, 'afterwards, when Jackson has been caught and the dust settles, we ought to get a programme with more bite in it than we expeced.'

'You've got something there. Like to bale out for a week or so?'

It was what I wanted to do – to take my baggage and fly back into the obscurity of London. I could hide there, not only from the ugliness that had invaded Kersivay but also from myself. This was my opportunity, while time remained.

As I stood there, holding the receiver, I glanced out through the glass panel of the call-box. At the reception desk Harringay was talking to Rona Carmichael. They were looking in my direction, and the girl's expression was one of puzzlement and even alarm.

And suddenly, in that split second, I realized that I must face the truth. For too long I had been expending nervous energy trying to avoid it. Now I must act. Now I must deliberately 'thole my assize', even though the decision might well have come too late.

'Hallo! Are you still there, Peter?'

'Yes. The line seems a bit dodgy.'

'Did you hear what I said? Like to bale out?'

'I'd rather stay, if that's all right with you. I could pay my own expenses until such time as I begin work on the programme—'

'Be your age, Peter! Don't be so ruddy independent!' His voice was warm and soothed me. 'Stay by all means – but for Pete's sake stop nattering about expenses. If anyone deserves a break you do!'

'Thanks,' I said.

'By the way, are you quite fit? You sound – well, "strained" is the word that comes to mind.'

'I told you, it's pretty grim here.'

'Of course. All right, Peter – keep in touch. Look after yourself.'

That was what I intended to do – look after myself. Cradling the receiver, I emerged from the call-box.

Harringay had gone. Behind the desk, Rona Carmichael appeared to be adding up figures in a ledger. The afternoon had become warm and sultry, and she was wearing a narrow-waisted print frock. It had a reddish pattern which suited her dark hair. She looked as fresh as a sea breeze. As comforting, too.

I wished I knew her better. Then I could have discovered, perhaps, what Harringay had been saying to her. More important, I could also have derived comfort from a mere exchange of intimate talk.

As I passed the desk she looked up. There was wariness in her eyes but also a kind of compassion.

'Is your headache better, Mr Parsons?'

I was surprised. And pleased, too, by her unexpected interest. The double shock made me stammer.

'Yes. Yes, quite better, thank you. But – how did you know—'

'Major Rivington-Keel told me about it – when he phoned this morning. So did Mr Harringay, a minute ago. I noticed you weren't looking too well yesterday, just after you arrived.'

'The fresh air helped,' I told her. 'When I joined the search-party I soon forgot all about it.'

'You should see a doctor. We used to get a number of people like yourself in hospital – actors, stage-directors, newspapermen, people constantly working to a deadline. They suffered from bad headaches – followed in some of the worst cases by short spells of amnesia. But in each case the cure was comparatively simple.'

I wanted to tell her about myself; but something – a secretive instinct, perhaps – made me hesitate.

I changed the subject. 'You weren't born in Kersivay?'

'No. In London.'

'So that's where you got the accent?' The aim was to sound flippant. 'I wondered if it might be a put-up job!'

The unexpected sunny smile which she'd inherited

from her grandfather came into being. It almost stopped my heart, because it was for me. Her front teeth were a shade irregular, giving her a mischievous, wholly feminine look which I found entrancing.

'A put-up job? Really, Mr Parsons! If you want to know, I'd give anything to acquire a Gaelic brogue. The guests would like it better, too.'

'Some of your guests.'

'Well' – she smiled again, this time more conventionally – 'it's not every day we get people from London like you and Mr Catford. And Mr Harringay.'

'So you worked in a London hospital?'

'St Luke's,' she said. 'My mother was the King's eldest daughter. The Princess Royal, Dad used to call her. He was a chartered accountant. He came on a fishing holiday to Kersivay and carried her off to live in Kensington. Five years later he was killed in the war, piloting a reconnaissance Hurricane in Burma.'

'Your mother is dead, too?'

She nodded, blue eyes clouding with tears. 'She died eighteen months ago, during the flu epidemic. That's why I came here, to help Granpa. I was doing all right in hospital, of course. But – but sometimes you want to be near your own kith and kin, Mr Parsons.'

'I know.' I remained staring at her, like a fool.

She flushed and said: 'This is a terrible thing that's happened to Kersivay.'

I came back to reality. 'No news of Jackson yet?'

'None. You'd think he'd have found it impossible to stay hidden for so long. On a small island like this.'

'Could he have got away by boat?'

'Granpa says it's unlikely. A boat couldn't operate

in the fog last night, and since the weather cleared the coastguards have been on watch.'

I had seldom met anyone so easy to talk to. I had no painful urge to be witty or smart, and after the brittle relationships I'd been used to in broadcasting, this gave me an unusual feeling of calm.

We must have stood there, talking, for nearly an hour. At times we digressed from the main subject of discussion.

We spoke about her grandfather and the ramifications of his power on the island.

'Sometimes I think he really likes being called the King,' she smiled. 'Particularly now he's getting old. It compensates for a loss of power in his muscles. He went to Germany last year – to a hoteliers' congress in Lübeck. I persuaded him to go, because he badly needed a holiday, not only from his work but also from Kersivay. When he came back I began to wish I'd never mentioned Lübeck! His great idea was to found a chain of hotels in the West Highlands, and I had quite a time of it trying to calm him down! Of course, he's back to normal now – and I've come to understand that even the nicest of men – like Granpa – can sometimes be obsessed by delusions of grandeur.'

'The Big Mick complex,' I said.

We spoke, too, of Murdo Cameron: of his quick enthusiasms and dislikes, of the odd violence of his temper when it was roused.

'I remember one night in the bar,' she said. 'He got into an argument with a visitor from Edinburgh – a rugby player who started making silly, derogatory remarks about shinty. Murdo struck him with his stick, and if it hadn't been for Granpa using his influence and smoothing things over, the case might have gone into court.'

'It's the Highland temperament,' I said. 'Murdo was always the same. In school he often just about flayed us alive, but we were never really afraid of him.'

I offered her a cigarette and lit it – sharply conscious as I leant across the desk of her smooth bare arms and the delicate perfume in her hair.

'He hates Terry Jackson and his kind,' she said.

'I know. That's the one thing I don't understand about Murdo. You may think it odd, Miss Carmichael, but I feel sorry for Jackson.'

'Why should I think it odd? I feel the same. He can no more help having those black-outs than – than you or I can help having measles.'

'But he kills.'

'We could kill, too, by inadvertently infecting others with disease.'

She was comforting. She was watching my face now, as if expecting a reaction that so far she hadn't got; but somehow this didn't worry me.

I said: 'And yet, even though I disagree with him in this, I'm fond of Murdo Cameron. If I met Jackson I'd probably detest him. Why is it we so often feel friendlier to the hale and hearty than to the sick?'

She touched my hand. 'That's a male point of view. Women don't share it.'

'I see.' I took a drag at my cigarette. Somewhat irrelevantly I added: 'The old folk of Kersivay would say Jackson was possessed by a devil.'

'Well, isn't it true? A devil simply personifies evil.' Her high-boned face became sad. 'The tragedy is that some of us are allowed the freedom of our wills to combat it, while unfortunate creatures like Jackson occasionally lose this advantage.'

Here our talk was interrupted.

Two of the guests – the Cockney Mr Catford and his young lady – came breezing in from a game of tennis, demanding cool drinks. Anxiety was far from their minds. A search-party had been organized: somebody else was doing the dirty work and the responsibility was not theirs.

As they collapsed, hot and laughing, into comfortable wicker chairs, the swing doors from the back premises opened to admit Nappy Neil. His red hair sprouted, though otherwise he looked smart enough in his long blue jersey.

Dispensing iced lemonade, Rona said: 'What is it, Nappy Neil?'

'Sorry to interrupt! I've brought your stamps.'

'Oh, good! I can get those bills out now.'

'I was wanting to talk to Peter – to Mr Parsons, I mean. There's – there's something I'd like to discuss with him.'

Tension returned to my body like a coiling spring.

6

Adventure with Nappy Neil

NAPPY NEIL led me out to the back. In the garden, some distance to our right, a few guests were sunning themselves in deck-chairs. Others played leisurely tennis.

We leant on a wooden gate leading into Willie Ross's farmlands. The sleek Ayrshire cattle which kept the hotel in milk lay in a ruminative circle only a few yards from us.

Quiet and secretive, Kersivay stretched away in front – the river and the village, *Glean nan Taibhis* and the swelling hills on either side. On the lower slopes of Unival I saw a line of moving dots which was almost certainly Sergeant McPhee's search-party.

Heavy clouds were gathering in the south-east, and hot puffs of wind came sighing down from the glen. Though apparently sluggish and calm, the sea behind us had developed a menacing growl.

In the meantime, cloud shadows chased each other across the fields.

The aspect of the island was always changing. Sunshine and clean Atlantic wind, fog and soaking rain – the weather of the Hebrides, variable as the mood of the Hebrideans. Myself included. Optimistic, pessimistic, in weather-glass rotation; eager for happiness, but suspicious of it, too.

Nappy Neil said: 'I went down to the airport as usual to meet the plane. There was nothing for the hotel, so on my way back I stopped at the shop to pick up a pair of shoes that Katie wanted.'

He was the leader. As had been the case when we were children, I allowed him to do the talking.

'Mrs Campbell was in – crying her heart out for Joanna but at the same time disturbed and curious about something that had happened only a few minutes before.'

'What was that?' I said quickly.

'Mr Harringay paid her a visit. He'd been there last night, waiting to see Joanna, but – well, as you know, she didn't come. This afternoon he asked if Joanna had a jewel-box. Mrs Campbell said she did have – and showed it to him. It was locked, but without even waiting for permission he forced it open with a knife. Inside they found a diamond brooch – and according to Mr Harringay it's worth a hundred pounds.'

'For Pete's sake!'

'Well you may say it! He advised Mrs Campbell to put it into a safe in the bank – and so she did. On her way home she came in to tell Katie's mother.'

'But was that all?' I asked. 'I mean, did Mr Harringay not say anything else?'

'He did, Peter. He said to Mrs Campbell: "I know what this is. I know where it came from. It's the evidence I've been looking for. I'll be able to tell you more about it – by tomorrow, I hope." Then he left, carrying his fishing-rod.'

'Mrs Campbell didn't notice which way he went?'

'She was too upset to pay any heed.' He arched his back, crossed his legs and brought his chin down to rest on his arms, which were folded on the top spar of the gate. 'Peter,' he said, 'there's something queer going on. I can feel it in my bones. Remember old Annie Mary this morning – what she was saying about the evil that has come to Kersivay. Maybe she's not so far wrong. Maybe Terry Jackson's escape is only part of it.'

A blackbird was carolling in a near-by clump of brambles. The air was so heavy that smoke from one of the hotel chimneys spread over us like a pall. It was peat smoke, pleasant to smell, tingling in the eyes.

'Big shots in the C.I.D. are coming from Glasgow,' Nappy Neil went on. 'They told me this at the post office, when I called for stamps for Miss Carmichael. Sergeant McPhee didn't phone for help until this afternoon, so they couldn't catch today's plane. But they're arriving first thing in the morning, by the steamer. They'll be finding out the truth of it then, I hope.'

'Did the reporters arrive – the newspapermen Murdo Cameron was telling me about?'

'Ay. Half a dozen at least. But Mrs Campbell will tell them nothing about the brooch. You can depend on that. She knows that if she did they'd be putting two and two together and dirtying Joanna's name. At the present moment they're with the search-party. I saw them going off to join it, in a car they'd hired from the garage. But I don't think they'll be getting much that's new.'

He glanced across at me, freckles prominent, eyes alight with inner excitement.

'Nappy Neil,' I said, 'this is not all you wanted to say to me. I know the signs. There's some kind of ploy building up in that head of yours.'

He grinned, sideways. 'The idea just occurred to me on the way back here from the village. Do you mind the old shaft in *Gleann nan Taibhis* – sunk by your grandfather for digging out the gold?'

'I certainly do. It just about ruined the old boy, because the vein soon petered out. But it was a godsend to you and me when we were kids. The very place for high jinks in wet weather.'

'That's right, Peter. Now don't you see what I'm getting at? After your grandfather gave up, the river changed its course and the entrance was hidden behind a waterfall. Folk forgot about it. But you and I – we found our way in by dodging behind the fall.'

I saw at once what he was getting at. 'You mean we should have looked into the mine this morning?'

'I think so.'

'I forgot it even existed,' I confessed.

'Exactly – like everybody else. Look,' he went on, standing upright and facing me, 'if they can't find Terry Jackson I bet that's where he is. In the old mine.'

'But – but the entrance is hidden.'

'Not now. Last year a big rock got stuck at the top and the waterfall swung a few yards to the left. Part of the entrance is right in the clear – that is, if the river's not in spate.'

Suddenly I understood what he was planning. 'If they don't find Terry Jackson before this evening, you think we should go and look there?'

'That's it, Peter. It would give us something to do. I hate just sitting back and waiting.'

The prospect of action – action that I'd been so anxious to initiate myself – began to relieve some of the tension inside me. But I was still worried about the ethics of the situation.

'The correct procedure would be to remind the police about the mine and suggest that they should do the job.'

'Ach, to hell with the correct procedure! This is for you and me, Peter – like in the old days when we had adventures.'

His language may not have been entirely boyish, but his enthusiasm certainly was. I felt myself responding to it.

I said: 'Admittedly the police wouldn't like to be sent on a fool's errand.'

'Just what I was thinking. Anyway, the Sergeant's bound to be dog-tired after being out all day. He'd be damned annoyed if he went stravaiging up the glen and found the mine empty.'

There were serious flaws in the argument, but I disregarded them. 'And if we should find nothing after all, nobody need know.'

'Exactly.'

I made up my mind. 'All right,' I said. 'It's a bargain.'

He punched my shoulder. 'I knew you'd be game for it! I'll bring a couple of torches.'

'Right. See you in the bar at seven-thirty. If Jackson has been caught before then – well, at least we can have a drink together.'

At seven-thirty I was waiting, with the same glow of anticipation that had always accompanied my outings with Nappy Neil in the past.

I had put on a couple of thick woollen jerseys and a pair of waterproof trousers over my flannels, for the threat of thunder had passed during the late afternoon, and a gale from the south was now rising, carrying spits of rain.

Willie Ross was serving in the bar. He had put aside sophistication and looked dour and anxious. He'd been in touch with Sergeant McPhee, he told me. The afternoon search-party had just returned, but without Terry Jackson.

'I cannot understand it!' he said. 'They've been through Kersivay with a toothcomb. They've spoken to everybody – farmers, shepherds, even the fisher-folk who live miles away at the back of Unival. Not a trace of him.'

Major Rivington-Keel came in, loudly demanding a double whisky and the latest news. When the King told him his stocky shoulders seemed to droop.

'But dammit, thing's impossible!' The scar gave a grotesque appearance to his mouth. 'Jackson must be somewhere.' Suddenly he leant on the counter and lowered his voice. 'Think anybody's hiding him?' he asked.

The King looked even more anxious. He said: 'I'm damned if I know, Major!'

For a time they eyed each other in silence. The guests at the small tables at the back stopped talking, too.

Then the Major gulped his whisky and put down his glass. 'Last night Joanna Campbell,' he said, deliberately. 'Whose turn tonight?'

In spite of the glow of Drambuie in my stomach, a shiver went through me. The other customers began to talk again; but it was nervous talk, without warmth or laughter.

'Ah, Parsons!' exclaimed the Major, becoming

aware of my presence. 'No headache tonight, eh? Where's Harringay?'

'Out somewhere.'

'He told us not to expect him back until late,' explained the King. 'Wouldn't be surprised if he didn't come in at all. A law unto himself, that one!'

'Spotted a man in the glen this afternoon. Fishing. Thought at first it might be Jackson, then realized this chap was nearly a foot taller. Wasn't lame, either.'

'That would be Mr Harringay. He took a rod.'

'Fishing! Dammit – at a time like this! Not scared, though – give him that.'

The door opened to admit a group of ruddy-faced young farmers who'd been out with the search-party. They were accompanied by half a dozen men in city suits and burberrys – men paler and somewhat older and with sharper eyes. The reporters, I guessed.

The bar echoed with loud conversation, and I retired from the counter. Though I'd spent a couple of hours before dinner napping in my room, I still felt tired – which was understandable, considering the events of the previous night. But lassitude was at once forgotten when I saw Nappy Neil at the door, silently beckoning. I finished my drink and joined him in the chilly dusk outside.

He handed me a stout walking-stick – a *cromak* – and a small electric torch.

'All set?'

'All set, Nappy Neil.'

The gale was screaming as we made our way by a short cut towards the mouth of the glen. As a solid base to its violin shrillness was the sea's continuous drum-roll. Every second the evening grew darker, but even in the mirk we could see in the distance white waves bursting above the rocks on the shore. When I licked my lips I tasted salt from the spray which flew inland.

We battled across open fields, and I got Nappy Neil to talk about himself. He strode easily against the storm, but I was out of condition and had to conserve my breath. Nevertheless, I enjoyed the one-sided conversation. The hard exercise and the atmosphere of clandestine adventure had a bracing effect.

He told me that his parents – who'd lived in a shepherd's cottage near the Big House – had died many years ago, soon after my mother and I had left the island. At first he'd been looked after by an aunt in the village; but now, after years of odd jobs – lobster-fishing, peat-cutting, road-mending, followed by a spell of National Service with the Black Watch in Germany – he had settled down to live in an annexe to the hotel as the King's general factotum.

He remained lively in mind and body, as in boyhood; but I could see that he had also acquired a worldly maturity a little surprising in a man who'd seldom been away from his native island. Given the educational advantages that I had enjoyed, for instance, he'd surely have gone far in any profession. Much farther than I had done. I wondered, however, if perhaps he was happier as he was – with a pleasant, sociable job which not only brought him a comfortable wage but also gave him the opportunity to indulge in leisurely reflection.

In any case, I kept thinking what a grand thing it was to be in his company again.

After an hour's slogging we reached the comparative shelter of the glen. High above us we heard the thunder of the gale, but among the hazels and brambles on the river-bank there was only a moderate breeze. Without Nappy Neil – and the occasional use of my torch – I should have been lost in this territory, though as a boy I had known every yard of it. Memory faded, however, and I no longer possessed the countryman's gift of seeing in the dark.

When I explained this to Nappy Neil he laughed. 'Eat more carrots, chum! And pick a country girl to go courting with. Then you'll have eyes like a cat!'

I was blowing a good deal, and I think he must have noticed this.

As we rounded a high knoll covered with gorse he stopped and said: 'Let's have a smoke. It's sheltered here. And the waterfall is still about a mile away.'

Gratefully I squatted down, leaning back against the gorse.

'Dammit, troops need a rest occasionally!' He gave a startling imitation of the Major's voice and manner. 'Good for morale!'

I laughed out loud, the first belly-laugh I'd had for a long time. 'You haven't lost your touch,' I congratulated him. 'Coming over in the plane yesterday I was remembering how you used to do old Annie Mary.'

He took one of my cigarettes. 'Ay, but I don't do her any more. It would be like making a fool of the Holy Mother herself.'

'Nappy Neil,' I said, accepting a light from him, 'I've got something to tell you. Something I've told to nobody else. As my oldest friend perhaps you'll be able to advise me what to do.'

In the darkness he wrapped his arms about his knees and stared at the tip of his cigarette. 'I thought there might be something,' he said. 'That's one of the reasons I suggested this ploy. To loosen you up. Out with it, Peter!'

I began at the beginning, with Myra, and went right through to the end. I told him about the blood on my hands after the first black-out, about the screams I'd heard – or thought I'd heard – the previous night.

When I finished he said: 'You're daft, Peter! There was no word of a body that first time, and a pound to a penny you got the blood off the steak in your fridge – groping about instinctively for something to eat when you came in. Last night was different. Maybe you did hear screams – maybe you just happened to be close to the scene of the murder. But if you're thinking you might have done it yourself – well, take it from me, man, it's impossible! Conscious or unconscious, you couldn't hurt a fly. I know. Do you mind the time you came crying to school because Roderick Dhu had drowned your kittens?'

'But psychopaths may be kind enough – in their lucid intervals—'

'I told you, Peter – don't be daft! You're not one of those. Plenty of folk have black-outs if they're mentally tired and under strain. The schoolmaster, for instance.'

'Murdo Cameron?'

'Ay. A year or two back, it was. He'd got into trouble with the Education Committee – about the eleven-plus exam. Murdo doesn't approve of it, and you know what he's like when he gets mad. He'd just lost his old housekeeper, too, and was waiting for his present one to arrive from the mainland. Joanna Campbell was doing a temporary job as his daily help, and she used to be telling Katie how sick he was. Once he took a bad turn in the hotel, and the King had to run him home in the station-wagon. But when Dr Barbour came he soon put him right. Tranquillizers and a month's holiday in Aberdeen. And look at him now – as healthy as a roe. Mind you, Murdo still isn't a bit grateful. He's always snarling away about the doc's new-fangled ideas.'

He was as comforting as Rona; and in any case, having unburdened my mind, I was beginning to feel a lot better.

'Maybe you've got something there,' I told him. 'The logical conclusion is that Jackson did murder Joanna Campbell.'

He threw away the stub of his cigarette. 'Just you relax, Peter, and have a blether with Dr Barbour. He's a bit of a yaw-yaw, and some folk don't like him, but he's good at his job.'

'Those words – *"Blackmail . . . nasty . . . barman"* – d'you think I imagined them?'

'Could be. Or they may have been used by Jackson, living in his evil world.' He got smartly to his feet. 'Come on,' he said, 'time we were moving. If we find Jackson in the mine the worst of your worries will be over.'

I scrambled up. 'You're not afraid of him?'

'Why should I be? He's a wee runt of a kid. I've seen him, you know – one time I was up at the prison with a message from the King to the Governor. You and I could make mince-meat of him.'

We resumed our march, picking a way with our torches through the bushes and the brambles.

After a time he said: 'If we do bring him in, Katie will be the first to thank us. She's terrible cut up about Joanna. She's afraid to leave the hotel, too –

even with me looking after her. But of course all the women are the same.'

'Does she know what you're doing tonight?'

'No fear! I just told her you and I were going out for a walk.' He laughed. 'She was inclined to be fussy in case we might meet the murderer – but pleased, too, in another way. Said you were a good influence, keeping me off the beer!'

Overhead a silver slice of moon dodged among the scudding clouds. The river on our left grew more turbulent as its bed narrowed and became steeper. It was hard work climbing along the sliding screes.

A smir of rain was blowing about us. On my face and hands sweat mingled with the moisture. Once or twice I had the notion that nothing was real – that a time-slip had put us back into some motiveless boyhood game. But the physical difficulties were generally enough to prevent too much introspection.

Then we heard the steady rush of the waterfall.

We climbed a rubbly mound, on which, even though wearing rubber-soled shoes, I found it difficult to keep my balance. Had we approached our objective from the upper part of the glen, the going would have been a lot easier. I remembered a grass-grown track in that direction, along which spoil from the mine had been taken in handcarts, first to a primitive washing-plant in the glen itself and thence to the Big House as top-dressing for the garden.

Finally the fall itself came in sight, a ghostly veil billowing down within a darkened stage. The sound of it made conversation between us almost impossible.

Nappy Neil went nimbly down a slope. I followed, more gingerly, flashing my torch.

We found ourselves on a rocky ledge, a couple of

yards wide, which raked inwards and upwards. In the old days it had been a tremendous thrill to move in behind the cascading water. Now we arrived at the entrance to the mine-shaft before we reached the fall.

It loomed up suddenly on our right, black and sinister, squared off with huge flat slabs of stone and less than eight feet square. As boys we had regarded it as a haunt of romance, an Aladdin's cave promising treasures as rich as our imaginations. Now it appeared to me simply as a dank tunnel, from which came an unpleasant smell of rotting vegetation.

We moved in a few yards, our feet sinking in loose gravel. The sound of the fall decreased in volume and became blurred in the background.

Nappy Neil shone his torch downwards.

On a bare patch of soft earth we saw a footprint. On the gravel round about it was a mark indicating that a heavy object had been dragged in across the threshold.

A bat flitted silently past my face, and I almost shouted in dismay.

7

Time's Lullaby

THE print was not clean-cut. It had been made by someone whose foot had slipped, probably in the act of pulling. A few yards farther in, too, the floor of the shaft became littered with heavy rubble, and there was no more chance of finding clear evidence. Even the drag-mark vanished.

There was a clatter above our heads. I ducked to avoid violent wings, and air stirred against my face.

'Wood pigeons,' said Nappy Neil. 'You can see their droppings.'

I made no reply, unwilling to betray the fact that I'd been considerably startled.

We moved on. The steady hiss of the fall faded into near-inaudibility, as if on some hidden panel a producer had been turning down the volume control. Of the storm howling in the hills we could hear nothing.

Some way in from the entrance, the shaft divided into two. Both divisions were slightly narrower than the main tunnel – perhaps by about a foot – but their height remained the same.

'Can you mind, Peter? It's the left-hand one that comes to nothing, isn't it?'

'Yes – after about fifteen yards. They found that the vein of gold curved off to the right.'

'You used to call it Disappointment Alley. The other was Gold Street.'

'And where we're standing now was Charing Cross. Well, Nappy Neil – which way?'

'No marks on the rubble hereabouts. Tell you what. You carry on down Gold Street. I'll have a dekko in Disappointment Alley and catch you up.'

'Right. Are we on to anything, do you think?'

'Somebody's been here. And not so long ago at that.'

I wasn't overjoyed about Nappy Neil's plan but made no objection to it, in case he might think I was afraid. As he went off to the left I entered the other tunnel.

I advanced slowly and carefully, spraying torch-light ahead of me, continually apprehensive of what it might reveal. Terry Jackson was 'a wee runt': Nappy Neil had said so. But I wasn't a giant myself – and what if the kid were armed? My only weapon was the *cromak* in my left oxter.

But all I saw was the slimy stone on either side; all I heard was the crunch of my own reluctant feet.

Once or twice I stopped. I wanted to listen. I also wanted to give Nappy Neil the opportunity to over-take me as soon as possible. But I could hear nothing definite.

There were small sounds, of course: the occasional drip of water from the roof, vague rustlings whose origins I couldn't guess at, the beat of my own pulses.

I decided to cough and clear my throat. Then I made my progress in the rubble heavy and noisy. I'd done the same thing twenty years before, on our first visit to the mine. Put up a brave front – that was the idea. If a ghost existed, scare it away.

A ghost? *Gleann nan Taibhis* – the glen of the ghost.

The story came back to me – the old ceilidh yarn whispered around the peat fires. The landing of the Norsemen, and the King of Kersivay's daughter ravished and abandoned by the blond Eric. But on his return to 'Norroway o'er the faem', the King's daughter had realized that her love for him was stronger than her hate. In the glen she would sing sad songs to his memory, and for very shame her father's folk had killed her.

But her spirit remained in the glen, and sometimes on a summer's day – or in the quiet of an autumn evening – her sad songs were still to be heard. All the old folk of Kersivay could sing them – Annie Mary McCuish, Maggie McLeod and many others. Murdo Cameron had written them down.

I shivered.

For the past minute I'd been standing in the same spot, but now I made another effort to go forward. Then it occurred to me that Nappy Neil was long in coming, and I stopped again to listen for sounds of his approach. None came.

I was sweating, the result of panic. For God's sake, Parsons, pull yourself together! You're a grown man, on serious business. Get shot of your Hebridean inhibitions, of all this romantic nonsense about a singing ghost! The only ghost is Terry Jackson, and—

'Peter! Peter!'

The voice was harsh, almost unrecognizable in the distance. Faintly I heard the echo of stumbling footsteps.

I turned and ran back along the tunnel. As I

reached the fork at Charing Cross a torch-light appeared, wavering, sagging.

'Peter! Where are you, Peter?'

'Here, Nappy Neil! What's the matter?'

He came close to me, panting, clutching my arm. 'My God! It – it's in there! I fell over it! I fell—'

'Hold it, now! Tell me about it.'

Illumined by both torches, his narrow face was so pale that the freckles stood out like the marks of a disease. But he fought down panic – panic that I understood only too well.

'Come and see, man!'

He dragged me round into Disappointment Alley. My shoes slithered in the deep rubble. I didn't allow myself to think at all.

He came to a halt. Our torches picked out the body of a man, lying at our feet.

A small man, and young, wearing only a grey flannel shirt and denim trousers soiled with earth. His mouth was open; his eyes stared into the light. Across his throat was a purplish weal, and his head had been pulled back almost at right angles to his spine. There was a bandage on his left ankle – a bandage which had been made by tearing a white handkerchief into strips.

I bent down. One half-clenched hand was stone cold. But as I touched it, the dead fingers began to open.

It was a stage in the passing of *rigor mortis* – I knew that. But the thing affected me so much that suddenly I had to turn aside and be sick.

The spasm passed.

'Who – who is it?' I said.

'Terry Jackson. I saw him once – I told you.'

'The murderer!'

'Ay. Seems he's been paid back.'

How long we stood there, staring, I don't know. The place was cold and desolate. No treasure, no ghost – only ugly, cruel death, with no romantic trappings. Death that was puzzling, however – an off-beat phrase in a rhythmic funeral march.

Nappy Neil's sigh had a quaver in it. 'What are we going to do, Peter?'

'I – I'm not sure. Better not move him, I suppose. Not until the police and Dr Barbour have seen him.'

'That's right.' He paused, rubbing his chin. Abruptly he said: 'Look, I could phone the police station from the Big House. It's less than a mile away, up the old track and straight across the moor. They could be here in half an hour – if they took a car, I mean, and came round by road to the top of the glen.'

I sensed what was coming and hated the thought of it. But I nodded and said: 'That's the best plan. You know the way.'

'Someone – someone's got to wait with the body.'

'I know. Someone's got to wait.'

'I mean, whoever did it might come back and—'

'Don't worry, Nappy Neil. I'll be all right.'

'I'd wait myself, but – I know the road—'

'Of course.'

'I'll go like hell. As soon as I phone I'll come back. Twenty minutes, Peter.'

'Sure.'

'It's five past nine now. Say twenty-five or half past.'

'Fine.'

'Got plenty of cigarettes?'

'I bought a new packet this morning.'

'O.K. Well – I'll beat it.'

I heard him stumbling towards the entrance. Then it grew quiet again, except for the faint, persistent sound of the fall.

Twenty minutes, he had said. Be your age, Parsons. Twenty minutes will pass. Everything passes. *Hush – 'tis the lullaby Time is singing – Hush, and heed not, for all things pass.*

But it was difficult not to heed the thing among the rubble at my feet. I moved away until I came to the junction of the tunnels. There I squatted down, back to the damp wall, and switched off the torch.

Fumbling, I found my cigarettes. I lit one and inhaled a lungful of smoke.

Ten minutes to a cigarette. I'd smoke two – slowly and carefully, one after the other. By the time I'd finished, Nappy Neil would probably be back. He'd go like hell. That's what he'd promised – and you could depend on Nappy Neil.

I switched on the torch. Up in the roof I saw bats hanging grotesquely from the stone slabs. So I switched it off again, in case the light should cause them to move.

I began to hum a song. *Play it cool, man – play it cool.. Don't scare the girl, man, that's the rule.* Soon it obsessed me. Over and over again I repeated the opening lines, until it became an automatic process, apparently independent of my will.

Self-hypnosis. One way of making the time pass.

Play it cool, man – play it cool. I'd used it once as a signature-tune in a programme about youth clubs in Birmingham. Not entirely successful in creating a pleasant atmosphere. Not entirely successful now — in the old mine, with Terry Jackson's maimed body lying only ten yards away.

Then the automatic process began to break down. My muscles stiffened. Reality overcame the anaesthetic qualities of the music. With explosive energy I flung away my cigarette, shone the torch on my wrist-watch.

Ten past nine.

I lit another cigarette.

There was a sound in Disappointment Alley – a rustling, a settling down. My shoes dug into the gravel. My back strained against the wall. But I didn't move or run away. I stayed there, smoking.

Time's lullaby had a slow and ponderous beat. Forget about Time, Parsons. Relax – that was Nappy Neil's advice. Relax. Fight away the first grim threat of another headache.

Relax. Use your brain to work out this new problem. *Play it cool, man – play it cool.* That's better. Consider the problem of evil that has come to Kersivay.

No headache now. It goes away if you forget about yourself. Forget about yourself – that's the cure.

This problem of evil – get it straight. Terry Jackson killed Joanna Campbell. But now someone has killed Terry Jackson. What's the logical conclusion?

The logical conclusion is that a second murderer remains at large. In Kersivay. No psychopath this time. Someone with a hard, cold reason for killing.

'The Unseen Killer'. That was the title of a programme I'd done on the 'flu germ. Now it fitted another subject. A person. A person who'd lured Terry Jackson to the mine, who'd killed him as he crossed the threshold and dragged his body into Disappointment Alley.

Motive?

Vengeance for Joanna Campbell? Blind hatred? A kill to prevent others being killed, like the A-bomb on Hiroshima?

Where was Kenneth Harringay?

Harringay. Why should I be thinking of Harringay at this time and of my cigarette-case in his pocket?

Again the rustle and soft suggestion of movement in the tunnel. I strained against the wall, jerked away my second cigarette. Switching on the torch, I looked at my watch.

Nine fifteen.

Something moved at my feet. I swung the torch. A wood pigeon clattered up, terrified, and flew out into the dark beyond the waterfall.

I put out the light and took another cigarette. My hands were so unsteady that I had difficulty in operating the lighter. But I made it. I made it and sucked in the smoke.

How had Terry Jackson died? His neck was broken: I was sure of that. He lay there, twisted – and so very still.

Except for his hand.

God, that had been a ghastly moment – when his fingers moved. What if he wasn't dead after all? What if even now, with a hideous rustling, his whole body was coming to life again, sorting itself out into a natural position, getting slowly to its feet?

This was madness. The turn of the screw, and the little dead children coming towards you, hand in hand. Relax. Relax. *'Yea, though I walk in death's dark vale—'*

That rustling sound. This time it wasn't coming from Disappointment Alley but from somewhere outside. A rustling, like footsteps on rubble.

Whoever did it might come back.

Whoever did it—

There was something. A movement. I got to my feet, breathing fast.

Someone on the ledge outside.

Nappy Neil can't possibly be back already. He's only been gone ten minutes. God, don't tell me it's in my imagination. Don't tell me it's the beginning of another black-out.

Make a noise. Cough. Thump your feet down on the gravel, Parsons. Advance. Don't run away. Don't ever run away again.

As I approached the entrance, I heard voices. Not one voice, but several. One of them was Nappy Neil's.

I took out my handkerchief and wiped sweat from my forehead. 'Who's there?' I called.

Nappy Neil came in, swinging his torch. 'Canny, Peter! I met Sergeant McPhee, Murdo Cameron and the doctor coming down the old track. Murdo was out posting letters in the village when he saw our lights flashing in the glen. Must have been after we stopped for yon smoke. He reported it to Sergeant McPhee, so they picked up the doctor – in case his hypodermic might be needed – and came round in the police car to investigate. When I told them what we'd found, Murdo went across to the Big House to pick up something we can use as a stretcher. And to phone the garage to send up a shooting-brake for the body. He'll be along in a minute.'

Scrambling, panting a little, Sergeant McPhee came into the light. He was in plain clothes, burly, fortyish, with broad clean-shaven jowls.

'Well, well, Mr Parsons, this is a terrible thing.' He didn't look me straight in the eye, which was curious, because I had the impression he was a straightforward man. 'Where is the body?' he inquired.

Nappy Neil said: 'I'll show you.'

As he conducted the policeman inside, I was joined by Dr Barbour. He wore a plastic mac which glistened in the beam of my torch.

'Why didn't anybody think about the old mine this morning?' His moustache bristled with efficiency and curiosity.

'I don't know.'

'Of course the prison people and Constable McKechnie, who are new to the island like myself, had probably never even heard of it.'

'Probably not.'

'Same with the younger folk. But the older inhabitants of Kersivay should have remembered.'

'It depends. Nappy Neil and I remembered it later on, but only because we used to play here when we were kids.'

'Sounds feasible. All right,' he went on, taking my arm, 'let's have a shufti.'

Sergeant McPhee had a flash-bulb camera. He made notes on the position of the body and took several photographs. Afterwards he searched the pockets of Jackson's denim trousers but found nothing. It was clear that in the absence of superior officers he was determined to be thorough in his duty.

Then Dr Barbour squatted down to make his examination. I noticed he used a clinical thermometer and paid close attention to the dead man's mouth.

During this initial post mortem Sergeant McPhee came and stood beside me, powerful and silent. I had a hemmed-in feeling – a touch, perhaps, of claustrophobia. And no wonder, in this dismal tunnel with Dr Barbour looking suddenly surprised as he noted down a reading from his thermometer.

The sergeant coughed. He said: 'Mr Parsons, what reason had you and MacDonald for coming here to-night?'

I had been waiting for this question. I had been dreading this question. Because, in fact, the answer I should have to give would be unlikely to satisfy a policeman.

'It – it's difficult to explain. We decided to have an adventure.'

'An adventure?'

'Yes. You see, Nappy Neil and I were boys together. We often played in here. It occurred to us that the mine was about the only place in the island that hadn't been searched.'

'Why didn't you let me know about it?'

'We ought to have done. But we knew you'd be tired after a long day, and – well, as I said, we wanted an adventure. We wanted to re-live the old days, if you see what I mean.'

'Why didn't you suggest looking in the mine this morning – when you were helping to search the glen?'

'The idea simply never occurred to me. Anyway, as we approached the waterfall, someone raised an alarm. Those of us on the left of the line had to scuttle across to help investigate a patch of whins. By the time we got going again, the fall was behind us.'

'H'm. But the idea occurred to you later?'

Nappy Neil had been listening. He said: 'The idea occurred to me, Sergeant. I mentioned it to Peter – Mr Parsons, I mean – and suggested this ploy.'

'Did you now?'

'Ay. But to tell you the truth, we never expected—'

He had to stop. A commotion occurred down the tunnel, and Murdo Cameron barged in, carrying a rolled-up stretcher.

'Roderick here found it in an outhouse. Relic of the Red Cross days during the war. Lucky his memory's good.'

Coming at his heels, Roderick Dhu passed just outside the glare of our torches. He nodded to me but gave the others no sign of recognition. His expression was secretive and grim.

'God!' The schoolmaster put the stretcher down and knelt by the body. 'The man's neck is broken!'

'Neat job,' observed the doctor, still fussing with his notebook.

'But – but look here, James – that's an old Nazi trick. Saw it in Germany many a time. Towards the end of the war, when they were panicking.'

'How d'you mean?'

'The weal on the throat. The Nazis killed a lot of political prisoners that way. A stick across the Adam's-apple and a knee on the upper spine. Then a jerk and a push – like thrawing a chicken's neck.'

'I see.'

'I was with the Seaforth's in the final attack on Lübeck – May 1945. When we captured General von Milch he admitted that the gas-chambers had become an expensive luxury and that more economical methods were being used.'

'You're probably right, Murdo.' Dr Barbour got slowly to his feet. 'But there's something else that's rather odd.'

Sergeant McPhee moved forward. 'Odd, Dr Barbour?'

'Yes. I cannot be positive, of course, until I make a thorough examination in the surgery, but I think Jackson has been dead for at least twenty-four hours. In that case he was murdered before Joanna Campbell.'

Somebody sighed. Sergeant McPhee, I think.

An echo rustled in the roof.

8

The Mark of the Beast

BETWEEN us, in the darkness, we carried the body up the glen and across the moor.

Out of the shelter of the banks of gorse and hazel, we could scarcely keep our feet in the gale. It howled in from the Atlantic, roaring and cracking in our ears, befuddling our senses. Every few minutes two of us had to stop, while another pair took over our burden. By the time we reached the main road, a few hundred yards from the Big House gate, we were all breathing fast like runners after a race.

The schoolmaster shouted in my ear: 'The tail-end of Hurricane Hetty, Peter. Heard about it in the news tonight. Likely to last for a couple of days.'

The police car stood in a lay-by. Flanking it was a shooting-brake, and as we manhandled the stretcher across a stile, the driver came running to help us.

When Nappy Neil addressed him as Lachie, I knew who he was at once. Lachie Robertson, the tough guy of the school, from whose ready fists Nappy Neil had often saved me. But now, in his tight leather jerkin, he bore no resemblance to a bully. He looked mild and small and insignificant.

He gave my arm a friendly squeeze.

Then, as we were about to put the stretcher and what it contained into the back of the shooting-brake, the lights of a car approaching from the direction of the village came leaping up over the moorland ridge.

'Who the hell—' began the schoolmaster.

'The reporters,' growled Sergeant McPhee. 'Or I'm a Dutchman.'

He was only partially right. As we lifted the stretcher and began to manœuvre it inside the vehicle the car dipped its headlights and drew up alongside. The others recognized it as Major Rivington-Keel's.

The Major himself stepped out, followed by a tall man of middle age, blond and bearded, who wore a belted mackintosh.

'Innes McInnes,' said the Major, without enthusiasm. '*Daily Gazette*. We were having a last drink together in the hotel when Miss Carmichael came in and told us what was happening. Message from the garage, apparently – which is run by the King's nephew.'

The fiery cross in the old days. The telephone in more modern times. News travelled fast in Kersivay. Especially to the ears of men like Willie Ross, whose interests and relatives were legion.

Innes MacInnes said nothing at first.

Above the noise of the wind, the Major inquired: 'Is it Jackson?'

Sergeant McPhee flicked on his torch and pointed. 'Have a look, sir.'

The Major bent down. I saw his brow wrinkle, his twisted mouth become more twisted still.

He nodded. 'It's Jackson all right.'

'I believe you were a prisoner of war in Germany, sir.'

'I was. But—'

'Seen that kind of killing before?'

'Sorry, McPhee. Don't get your meaning.'

'Mr Cameron says it was a Nazi method. Stick on the throat – knee in the back. I wondered if you'd come across it as well, sir.'

'Can't say I did. In hospital most of the time, though. Wounded.' He pointed to his mouth. 'At the same time could believe anything of the Nazis.'

Helping Roderick Dhu with the stretcher, the schoolmaster snapped: 'You've said it, Major!'

'So far it's only a theory, of course,' put in Dr Barbour, reminding authority of its dependence on professional skill. 'I'll do a comprehensive post mortem as soon as we get to the village.'

The double doors of the shooting-brake were slammed shut. Lachie Robertson went round to start the engine.

Our group was about to break up when Innes MacInnes spoke at last, addressing himself to Sergeant McPhee. 'So it's murder again?' he said.

'It's murder again, Mr MacInnes.'

'Some story! Are you handling the case yourself?'

'In the meantime. An inspector and sergeant from the Glasgow C.I.D. are due to arrive in the morning. By steamer.'

'If Hurricane Hetty doesn't ease down a bit there will be no steamer.'

'Well?'

The big reporter shrugged. 'O.K. by me,' he remarked, pacifically.

We sorted ourselves out. Sergeant McPhee and Dr Barbour climbed into the shooting-brake beside the body. Nappy Neil volunteered to drive the police car, taking as passengers Murdo Cameron, Innes MacInnes and myself. Satisfied that his help was not required, the Major decided that he and Roderick Dhu should return in his car to the Big House.

I was crouching in the shelter of a clump of brambles by the roadside, trying to light a much-needed cigarette, when I became aware of someone behind me. I stood up and made out the spare figure of Roderick Dhu.

He came closer, putting his mouth to my ear. 'Did you see it, Mr Parsons?'

'See what?'

'The mark of the beast.'

'What on earth d'you mean, Roderick?'

'The mark of the beast – on the dead man's throat.'

His voice had a hollow ring. His drawn, white face stared at me out of the mirk – the face of an Old Testament prophet crying woe unto sinners. The whole effect should have been funny; but instead of making me smile, it set my muscles quivering.

A few yards away the Major shouted: 'Roderick, where the hell are you?'

'I will have to go.' He touched my arm, and in spite of the circumstances – or perhaps because of them – I was convinced of his sincerity and friendly purpose. He said, quickly: 'Nineteenth Revelation, nineteenth verse. Take care, Mr Parsons. Take care.'

He left me, shambling away with bent shoulders.

I turned my back to the wind and this time, though my hands were unsteady, managed to light the cigarette. I needed it more than ever, because Roderick had given me an inkling of the truth. Somewhere in Kersivay a beast was lurking – a beast filled with what old Annie Mary had called 'the evil of arrogance'.

On the way down the winding road to the village, while violent gusts of wind plucked at the car and made Nappy Neil's job at the wheel a tricky one, Innes MacInnes kept up a monotonous barrage of questions. It was his good fortune that at nine o'clock, when his colleagues decided to return to the village, he had remained in the hotel bar talking to the Major. As a result – granted a good telephone line – he now had a scoop. It seemed that he meant to make the most of it.

He appealed to the schoolmaster. 'Mr Cameron – between ourselves – have you any idea who killed Terry Jackson?'

'Good grief, I don't have a clue! And if I had, d'you think I'd tell you?'

'In the circumstances, perhaps. Matter of policy—'

'Be your age, man!'

'Well, look – it's being said all over the island that Jackson must have had assistance in order to escape. Otherwise he couldn't have done it. Now then, I'd say whoever helped him over the prison wall is probably the killer.'

'Are you a University man?'

'No. But—'

'You'd never have got away with a proposition like that in the Logic class! Tell me, why should anyone take the risk of helping a man to escape and then coolly break his neck?'

'I don't know, Mr Cameron. But I've got a hunch—'

'Ach, you newspapermen! You and your hunches!'

'They work out sometimes. Lord Northcliffe said he always trusted his instinct more than his reason.'

None of us told him about Dr Barbour's tentative conclusion – that Jackson had been killed before Joanna Campbell. For the time being we were hiding it in the dark corners of our minds, reluctant to face the implications.

The other reporters were waiting outside the doctor's house, in the company of a few silent villagers. Faces were pale and intent in the light from a lamp standard. Coats billowed and flapped in the gale sweeping savagely down the street.

While Sergeant McPhee and Lachie Robertson carried the body inside, the rest of us were caught in a clamour of voices, all pleading for answers to many questions. On the sergeant's reappearance, the clamour increased.

At one point I glanced towards the post office. In a lighted kiosk Innes MacInnes was busy with the telephone.

Presently, however, the sergeant held up his hand. 'That's all we can give you tonight. When Dr Barbour completes his post mortem we may have a bit more to work on.'

He strode off towards the police station, and the reporters dispersed quickly, seeking telephones. Dr Barbour went into his surgery. Murdo Cameron said good night to us in a voice that for him was strangely quiet.

We were left in an awkward group around the two vehicles – Nappy Neil, Lachie Robertson, some men from the village and myself.

We had little to say to one another. The wind was so strong that we had to raise our voices to make ourselves heard, and Nappy Neil and I at any rate were almost too tired to shout. But there was something else – a constraint amongst us, the cause of which was not too difficult to analyse. For the past twenty-four hours it had been supposed that a convicted murderer was on the loose. The folk of Kersivay had been united in a common fear, especially when the news of Joanna Campbell's death became known. But now the convicted murderer was dead, and an unconvicted murderer remained at large: an unknown murderer who might be your neighbour – who might, in fact, be yourself.

I tried to talk and behave normally; but I was thankful when Nappy Neil arranged that Lachie Robertson should return the police car to the garage across the street and then run us both back to the hotel in the shooting-brake.

The King and Rona Carmichael were waiting when we went in. They took us to the kitchen, away from some guests who still lingered in the hall, and gave us food to eat. I forget what it was – roast-beef sandwiches, I think. But afterwards we drank whisky and strong sweet tea, and I for one felt less shaky. Rona kept watching my face, her eyes anxious.

Nappy Neil told the story.

As he finished I looked at Rona and dragged the ugly truth into the open. 'There's something you ought to know. Dr Barbour says he's not certain about it, but I don't believe he'd have mentioned it unless he was. He thinks Jackson was killed some hours before Joanna Campbell.'

'Good grief!' said the King.

I noticed his hands – big powerful hands writhing and twisting together between his knees. I noticed, too, that life seemed to have drained from Rona's face, leaving it colourless and infinitely sad within its halo of black hair.

Willie Ross said: 'What do you make of it, Peter?'

But the answer came from Nappy Neil. He was no

longer the brisk adventurer. He looked older – harder too, and burdened with knowledge.

'There's only one thing anybody can make of it! Some person wanted Joanna Campbell out of the way – so he thought out a plan. He posed to Jackson as an ally and told him to be ready for the first thick fog. Then he helped him to escape, led him to a pre-arranged hideout in the mine and killed him there. A few hours later this unknown person killed Joanna, knowing fine that Jackson would get the blame for it and that no awkward inquiries would be started. He probably meant to bury Jackson's body at the first opportunity, some place where it might never be found. A clever idea – but he didn't reckon that the mine would be searched so soon. His plan went haywire, and I'm willing to bet that like Burns's mouse there's a panic in somebody's breastie tonight.'

'This – this murderer – why should he burden himself with such a complicated plan? Couldn't he simply have killed Joanna and hidden *her* body?' The King's hoarse voice was almost supplicating.

'In that case he'd have risked awkward inquiries just the same. No, he believed that Jackson's escape – and disappearance – would be his insurance policy.'

After a silence, Rona said: 'It's too horrible! And out of character – in Kersivay, I mean. We could kill in anger, or for love. But never with such cruel calculation.'

'Unless it was done by someone not quite sane,' I said.

They looked at me sharply, all three of them.

'No!' exclaimed Nappy Neil.

And the King put a hand on my knee. 'Out of the question, Peter. This murderer has all his wits. He is ruthless and determined, and at all costs we must find him.'

Shortly before midnight I accompanied Nappy Neil to the back door, as he made his way to his room in the annexe across the open courtyard. In the corrider he paused.

'I think I know what's going on in that daft head of yours, Peter. But it's impossible – the whole damned thing's impossible, as I told you before. If you'd just relax and use your loaf, you'd see that it's impossible!'

'I expect you're right,' I said.

'Of course I'm right.' Suddenly he grinned. 'Lachie Robertson's not such a bogy now, is he?'

'Just what I was thinking. But—'

'There's a moral in the tale. Everything depends on the point of view.'

He opened the door and with a wry 'Good night' disappeared into the storm.

I went up to my room feeling so tired that for a time I lay on top of the bed with a mind that was almost blank. But the roar of the wind outside seemed to grow stronger, and in the end the rattling of the window forced me to get up and fasten the catch.

I began to undress. The hotel was full of sounds – creakings and small rustlings caused by the gale. The sea thundered in the distance.

Pulling on my pyjama trousers, I left the jacket off and filled the wash-basin with cold water. Then I splashed my face and neck and gave myself a towelling.

But this treatment did not make me forget. Nothing would make me forget those two warnings – the warning that seemed to lurk in Rona's blue eyes and the warning uttered by Roderick Dhu in the loud darkness of the moor.

Nineteenth Revelation, nineteenth verse. Take care, Mr Parsons. Take care.

I know my Bible fairly well. My father was an elder of the Kirk, and though in the past few years I'd neglected religion – to my disadvantage – memories of texts learnt in Sunday School often came back to me. But what the nineteenth chapter of Revelation was about I had no idea.

In some Scottish hotels Bibles may be found in the top drawer of the commode. Not here, though. But I believed there would be one in the big book-case in the hall.

It was now one o'clock, and it seemed likely that the staff and guests would be in bed. I put on my dressing-gown, therefore, and in my slippers opened the door and went quietly downstairs. I badly wanted to read that chapter.

I still had the torch that Nappy Neil had given me, and it was a necessary aid in the darkness of the hall. Carefully I made my way across the thick carpet, past the table and telephone boxes.

As I reached the book-case I noticed a bar of light beneath the door marked *Private* which flanked the reception-desk. This didn't worry me. Probably either Rona or her grandfather had found work to do after Nappy Neil and I had gone.

I ran the torch-beam along the rows of books.

Romances, crime novels, paperbacks, tomes of Scottish history; one slim volume entitled *The Story of Kersivay* by John Parsons – a labour of love by my father, completed just before the war and published at his own expense.

More books by John Parsons; novels this time, the royalties from which he had hoped would supplement his income from the estate. *The Sea of Glass, Blood in the Heather, Sigh of the Wind* – titles I remembered well. Knowing that my mother had no interest in his writing, he had often discussed their plots with me, for literary ideas and enthusiasms have to be shared with someone – and even a child is better than nobody.

An edition of Burns. *The Phoenician Origin of the Britons, Scots and Anglo-Saxons,* by Professor L. A. Waddell. *The Journal of a Tour to the Hebrides with Samuel Johnson,* by James Boswell.

Kersivay, I remembered, was visited by Johnson and Boswell in the autumn of 1773, in weather described as 'stormy and inclement', which seems to prove that September in the island has always been chancy, meteorologically speaking. They spent a night at the Big House, being entertained by a Parsons of the period. The meal was so elegant that it reminded Johnson of England, 'which made him uncommonly happy', Boswell, however, became considerably drunk and brought upon himself a rebuke from the doctor. Having few contacts with the outside world, the natives were 'highly ignorant and superstitious', and the tippling Scots lawyer, to his obvious delight, learned about *Glean nan Taibhis* – translated by him as 'the ghostly glen'. He noted, too, 'a fearsome cliff of sandstone, the Hirsay Cliff, from which, in former times, thieves and harlots were thrown to their deaths'.

I raised the torch-beam. More paperbacks. *Aftermath in Europe* by Albert van Kramer. Twelve volumes of an encyclopaedia.

Then at the end of the top shelf I spotted the Bible, a hefty edition bound in leather. I stretched up to pull it out. As I brought my arm down, the sleeve of my dressing-gown caught the pile of paperbacks. They overbalanced and slithered to the floor, making a considerable noise.

Bible and torch in one hand, I began to pick them up; but before the last one was in place the private door opened, sending a ray of light across the hall. I stood within it, blinking.

The main chandelier was switched on, and I saw Rona.

9

Two Kinds of Revelation

'MR PARSONS!' she said.

'I – I'm sorry if I disturbed you. I was looking for a Bible.'

A gust of wind savaged the front door. She, too, was in a dressing-gown. She wore no make-up and her hair was tumbled, as if she'd been lying down.

She came forward and said: 'I thought it might be Mr Harringay.'

'Harringay?' I put out the torch and slid it into my pocket. 'Hasn't he come back from fishing?'

'Not yet. But he told Grandpa he mightn't be in until the small hours of the morning.' She sat down on the arm of an easy-chair, shoulders drooping under thin silk. 'Peter,' she said, 'I'm worried.'

'That's only natural. Everybody is.'

I felt awkward, inadequate. With one thumb I kept flicking at the pages of the Bible.

'It's not just about – about what's happening now. Last time Mr Harringay was here he often stayed out late. Sometimes he didn't show up until the next day, and he never told us where he was.' After a momentary hesitation she added: 'Then – then *you* didn't come in last night.'

My fingers clamped on the cold leather. 'How – I mean, I didn't think you knew about last night.'

'I knew. I put a hot-water bottle in your bed about ten o'clock. Because of the fog. When Major Rivington-Keel phoned up this morning to say you wouldn't be in for breakfast I went to your room and found the bottle in exactly the same part of the bed I'd put it in.'

So much for my hopes of keeping a secret.

I said: 'I *was* out.'

She looked up at me, her eyes unhappy and even a little angry. 'For a long time something has been going on that I don't understand. Kersivay is different from what it used to be – overlaid with ugliness and suspicion. Suspicion of one's friends, of one's neighbours. And now, of course – now it's all much worse, and I – I didn't expect you to be a part of it. The Parsons were fine people. Real island people. I was brought up in that belief. But now—' Suddenly she stopped. 'Forgive me,' she said, putting a hand on my sleeve. 'I'm not like my grandfather. I allow my tongue to rattle on.'

'I'm not a fine man,' I said and dropped the Bible on the table.

She moved from the chair and bent down to stir life into the remains of a fire in the grate. I knelt beside her, took a peat from the fuel-bin and placed it on the red ashes. Tiny sparks were immediately sucked up the chimney, out into the gale.

'What do you mean?' she said, sitting on the rug and tucking her legs beneath her.

I sat down, too. Her face appeared younger and more delicate than it had done in the daytime. Her expression was grave and had none of the gloss of the professional receptionist. It struck me as betraying innocence and even vulnerability. The low neck of her dressing-gown revealed the shadow between her breasts. But it was a shadow as innocent of artifice as her expression.

'You might as well know,' I said. 'There was a girl in London. I was her lover – in every sense. But it turned out that she didn't love me, except perhaps in one sense, and in the end she married somebody else. I got worked up about it and began to have headaches and black-outs. What happens to me during those black-outs I just don't know. I had one last night, up near the old sea-weed factory. Just before I passed out I think I heard a woman scream. When I came to myself this morning I was lying in the bracken near the top of the Hirsay Cliff.'

She looked at me. She might not have the dourness of her grandfather, but her eyes were steadier than his.

'Thank you for telling me,' she said. After a pause she continued: 'I'm sorry about what happened, Peter. That – that girl, I mean. But as far as your physical trouble is concerned – well, I told you this afternoon that I've often seen cases like yours in hospital. A few tranquillizers, a good long holiday – perhaps a tonic – that's all you need.'

'Then you don't think—'

'That it's something more serious?' She shook her head, slowly. 'Poor Peter. It gets all bottled up inside you, doesn't it? But there's nothing at all to worry about: I'm certain Dr Barbour would confirm this. You have none of the characteristics of a – of a psychopath, and people with experience can always tell a psychopath by his eyes. Your eyes are – well, your eyes are kind' – she smiled a little – 'even when you look at me like that.'

'Rona, you can't tell what a relief it is to hear you say it.'

'I think I can tell.' The peat blazed, putting rosy colour in her cheeks. 'In the meantime you must face up to things – give yourself a chance.'

'A chance?'

'Peter,' she said, 'what were you doing last night – at the sea-weed factory?'

'I left the bar to be sick – and to go and see Dr Barbour. About my headache. But in the fog I lost my way.'

'I see.'

'Something else happened. I dropped my cigarette-case up there and Harringay found it.'

'You've really got problems, haven't you?'

'I know. This afternoon – when we were talking – I thought of asking for your advice.'

'I could almost tell.' She smiled again. 'You were like a wee boy, wanting to tell his mother something but afraid of how she might react.'

'Perhaps,' I said.

She turned and looked into the blaze. 'You brood too much,' she told me. 'And coddling will never cure that. Maybe you need to be shocked out of thinking so much about yourself and your personal problems.'

'But, Rona, you just said—'

'You also take yourself too seriously. A sense of humour is a healthy thing.' She must have noticed that I'd taken a metaphorical splash of cold water full on the face, because she leant closer and smiled, removing all possible traces of unfriendliness. 'That time in London,' she said, 'had you been drinking?'

'Pretty heavily.'

'To forget – the girl?'

'Yes.'

'There you are. You were tight. Looking at it from your point of view at the time, the thing was a tragedy. But now, from another point of view, couldn't it have been a comedy?'

I laughed. I couldn't help it.

'What a wonderful nurse you must have been,' I said.

'Pretty average, really.'

'You're right, you know. I *have* been taking myself too seriously. For the past six months I've thought of nothing but myself. I'd even become convinced I was ready for a psychiatrist's couch, God help me! The trouble was—'

'That you hadn't anybody to talk to about it. I know, Peter. I'm Highland, too, though I was born in London. I'm another sucker for the Celtic twilight.'

'I don't believe it!'

'It's true. I've done my share of brooding – over a certain man. And also been on the verge of a nervous breakdown. I suppose – I suppose that's why I recognized the signs in you and can sympathize. But when my mother died the shock helped to cure me. When I came back to Kersivay and friends treated me as an ordinary mortal and not as the heroine of a Shakespearian tragedy – when they laughed and kidded me out of myself – the cure was completed. I'm a saner being now – I think.'

The fire was warm. The turmoil of the wind outside made it seem even warmer, its comfort more intimate. The hotel was quiet. We were alone, vulnerable to each other.

As we continued to talk, a feeling of tenderness

came to me. I needed her, because she was comforting and kind and desirable. I needed her, because I realized suddenly that she also needed me.

After a time I said: 'So you have been in love as well?'

'I thought I was. A doctor in the hospital. Of course he was married. It's such a trite story I can scarcely believe it happened to me.'

'He must have been a swine! No one but a swine would ever try to take advantage of you, Rona.'

She smiled. 'What exactly do you mean?'

'You're so – so—'

'So innocent?'

'Yes.'

She shook her head. 'Perhaps I took advantage of him. However, it's over now. And I'm glad. You should be glad, too – to be rid of someone you couldn't trust.'

'That's a way of looking at it.'

'Isn't it the only way of looking at it? Could you sleep with your girl now – now that you know she doesn't love you?'

'No.' Oddly enough, thinking about it didn't hurt. 'No, I don't think I could.'

'Love is indivisible. So I want to believe. Physical and spiritual, both interacting. Don't you agree with me?'

'I'd like to agree with you. But I don't know. Every day you read or hear of something which appears to prove the opposite.'

'Yes, I suppose so. But we must have an ideal, mustn't we? Without an ideal we think of nothing but ourselves, like animals.' She stopped. 'What am I saying!' she exclaimed. 'I'm sorry. I – I scarcely know you, and yet—'

'And yet it's so easy to talk to each other.'

'Do you feel that, too?'

Her hand rested on the tiled fender. For answer I covered it with mine.

She said: 'Don't let's ever give up our ideals. Or try to rationalize them. If we hide the truth within ourselves, I think the result is often ugliness and shame.'

'Sometimes revelation hurts too much.'

'Not in the long run. Not if it comes through love.'

'Or through a sense of humour?'

'Or through a sense of humour.' She smiled and took my hand in both of hers; then her expression changed. 'But sometimes we must also be serious. Peter,' she said, 'I have to tell you. I'm not the only one who knows you were out last night.'

The happy interlude was ending.

I said: 'Who else does know?'

'Fiona Kennedy – the chambermaid. She made your bed after you slept in it yesterday afternoon. And turned down the covers. That was before I put the hot-water bottle in. But this morning she and I went into your room together, and she saw the bed just as it had been the night before. Fiona's boy friend is Constable Anderson. She'll tell him when she sees him tomorrow.'

'I see.'

'Before she does, you must tell the police yourself – if only to resolve the tension in your own mind.'

'You mean – tell them everything?'

'Everything. Face up to it, Peter. Not only for your

own sake, but also because Kersivay needs the truth. And you're a Parsons, to give us the truth.'

'The truth may be uglier than anyone imagines.'

'I know.'

She got to her feet, supple and tall. I stood close, aware of her body under the silk of her dressing-gown.

I think we must have remained like that for some time. I don't remember. All I know is that in those few seconds the relationship that had been established between us became more than a mere relationship, and worldly wisdom perished in the blaze.

'There's something else I must face up to,' I said.

'What is that?' She didn't look away, but her breast rose and fell as her breathing quickened.

'I love you,' I said.

She wasn't surprised or nervous or shocked. We had known each other for less than thirty-six hours, but those hours had been packed with danger and emotion, and it was enough.

'Oh, Peter!' was all she said.

Then she came to me without hesitation, pressing taut and strong, her kisses as eager as mine. I held her close, conscious only of a wild happiness and strength.

At lat, breathless, she leant back a little, putting one hand against my cheek. 'How – how did it happen?' she whispered.

'I don't know. It's like a miracle. Rona – you are beautiful.'

'I'm not, but I'm glad you think I am.'

'I can't believe it: that – that you love me. I love you, darling. I need you. But – but—'

'But you'll wait?'

'Yes. Until you decide.'

'Peter, I can't believe it has happened like this,

either. There's nothing complicated about it at all.'

'Not a thing.'

We kissed each other, love and desire indivisible. Somewhere in the hotel a clock chimed once. She moved out of my arms.

'I must go.' Her smile came with its power to make my heart turn over. 'I know what we both want, but it can't be – not yet.'

'Of course not.' I took her hand and kissed it. 'I'll care for you all my life.'

She stood on tip-toe and kissed me again. 'I knew,' she said. 'I knew what you were really like, darling. She hadn't a clue, poor thing.'

I didn't even wonder what she meant. It didn't matter. For a moment she stood haloed in the light of the door marked *Private*. She blew me a kiss. Then the door shut, and I was alone in the hall.

As I picked up the Bible and went upstairs I found myself whistling. In my room I took off my dressing-gown and got between the blankets, keeping only the bed-light on. I was new and clean and happy.

But for Rona's sake the truth had still to be uncovered. The truth about the death of Joanna Campbell. The truth about Kersivay. Tomorrow I would see the police – and the C.I.D. men when they came.

The truth. The whole truth and nothing but the truth. It couldn't harm me now. The shadows in my mind were imaginary. I had Rona's word for it.

I opened the Bible at the nineteenth verse of the nineteenth chapter of Revelation.

I read:

And I saw the beast, and the kings of the earth, and their armies, gathered together to make war against him that sat on the horse, and against his army.

And the beast was taken, and with him the false prophet that wrought miracles before him, with which he deceived them that had received the mark of the beast, and them that worshipped his image. These both were cast alive into a lake of fire burning with brimstone.

I remembered the gaunt, white face of Roderick Dhu. Did he know something about the beast? Or had his warning been simply a vague, Calvinistic reaction to evil?

That night I didn't concern myself with the problem for long. I had Rona to think about.

I put out the light and listened comfortably to the clamour of the gale.

Just before I fell asleep I thought I heard the sound of a car receding in the distance.

10

Essay in Production

I WOKE up to Rona's kiss. She was bending over, shaking my shoulder.

'You *are* a lazybones, darling! It's almost half past eight.'

I pulled her down and kissed her. No surprise, no awkwardness.

'I love you,' I said.

She laughed and disengaged herself. 'This is an absolute scandal, you know! In a respectable hotel. But I've brought you a cup of tea to provide myself with an alibi.'

I sat up. She was wearing a white blouse, navy blue slacks and a Fair Isle cardigan. Her eyes were astonishingly bright.

'Sugar and milk?' she said.

'One spoonful of sugar. Just a dash of milk.'

She smiled. 'I'll have to remember that.'

I struggled to emerge from a smug and silly happiness. I heard the wind.

'Darling,' I said, 'what's the day like?'

'The gale is blowing as hard as ever. I listened to the eight o'clock forecast and Hurricane Hetty is still on our doorstep. But they promise she'll move away by afternoon.'

I took a sip of tea. We kept looking at each other, as if we had all day to do it in.

Finally she sighed and said: 'I'll have to go, Peter. There's so much to do. But – but you'll go to the police after breakfast?'

'Yes. Any news of Harringay?'

'He's still out. I – I'm not sure what to do about it. In the circumstances, I mean. But Grandpa says he is well able to look after himself.'

The sadness had come into her face again. I did my best to dispel it.

'I'm sure the King is right. After all, Harringay's a grown man.' I caught her hand and said: 'Thank you for the tea, darling. You look lovely.'

She recovered her smile. 'You look quite nice yourself, even though you do need a shave!' And as I kissed her again she added: 'My chin feels – well, I think "lacerated" is the word. I bet Katie and Fiona and all the others are going to notice it!'

When she left me I gulped down the tea and got up, filled with a sense of purpose. It was a good feeling: an invigorating feeling after months of depression.

Downstairs I saw neither Rona nor her grandfather. Some time soon it would be necessary to tell the King that I wanted to marry the Princess; that I intended to carry her 'o'er the faem' – not to Norroway, of course, but almost equally as far to London. I had a feeling that his reaction might prove to be distinctly tough.

But before such an interview could take place I had to make certain of many things. Including the reason for Harringay's absence.

In the dining-room Katie served me with porridge and grilled sea-trout.

'How's Nappy Neil this morning?' I said.

'He is well. But it was a dreadful thing you did last night – you and him. You must be careful, both of you.' She was on the verge of tears. 'Who is it, Mr Parsons? Who is this – this murderer?'

'I don't know.'

'If you go prying too much – you and Nappy Neil—' She stopped there, leaving the possibility unspoken.

'Don't worry, Katie. The police will find out who it is. Remember the C.I.D. men are coming today.'

'They're not,' she said.

In spite of the wind, so far the morning was free of clouds, and sunlight glinted on the napery and silver. The murals shone with a sense of peace not reflected in the turbulence of the seascape framed in the big windows. Most of the guests had finished breakfast. Only two old ladies still lingered over their coffee.

'You mean—'

'I mean they can't come. The post office phoned Mr Ross a few minutes ago to say the steamer has been cancelled this morning. The afternoon plane as well. I knew fine they could never face it in this weather.'

'Well, it doesn't matter. I'm sure Sergeant McPhee and the two constables are perfectly capable of doing the job by themselves. If we all help.'

'That's the trouble. Some of us will help and others won't. And those who do help may get hurt. Nappy Neil knows that. I – I could tell he was afraid by the way he kissed me this morning.'

Afterwards I went out to the garage at the back and found him tinkering with the engine of the station-wagon. His sandy hair looked as if it had never seen a comb.

I said: 'I'm on my way to the police station. To tell them what happened two nights ago, up at the sea-weed facory.'

'That's a good thing, Peter.'

'Rona thinks it's a good thing.'

'I see.' He smiled a little to himself, but his underlying mood was serious. 'I suppose you've heard the C.I.D. men are not coming today?'

I nodded. The gale rattled the doors and shrieked across the corrugated iron roof.

'The priest and the minister have organized a joint service,' he told me. 'Twelve o'clock in the village hall. To pray for Kersivay's deliverance.'

'Protestants and R.Cs together!'

'Ay. An unusual thing in this island.'

'Death has no particular brand of religion, I suppose.'

He wiped his fingers on a piece of rag. 'I'm going down to the shop in a minute for some groceries. I'll take you along if you like and you can talk to Sergeant McPhee before the service.'

'Thanks. I wasn't looking forward to battling against that wind on my feet.'

By the time we were half-way to the village clouds had begun to obscure the sun. A rain-squall lashed against the windscreen. Nappy Neil was forced to slow down.

'What happened last night after I left you?' he inquired casually, peering forward as if I weren't there.

'I had a long talk with Rona.'

'You're looking different, Peter. I'm glad.'

The rain squall cleared. In a field on our right,

sheltered on three sides by a plantation of firs – trees grown by my father to protect pheasants and grouse in winter – a farmer in black oilskin coat and trousers was gathering in a flock of cross-bred sheep. Murders might be committed, a smell of fear might overhang the island; but animals must be tended even though human affairs are in turmoil.

The wind was blowing from the farmer's direction and even above the drone of the station-wagon's engine we could hear him whistling commands to two slender black and white collies. Commands which grew louder and more insistent.

But for some reason the collies were paying no attention to him – which was odd, because this breed produces the keenest and most biddable dogs in the world. Instead of racing to obey his instructions, they were scrabbling furiously under the wall of the sheep-fank which stood just ahead of us, in a corner of the field close to the road.

'Old Hector will be mortified that we saw this,' said Nappy Neil, grinning. 'These are the dogs that always win the Kersivay sheep-dog trials. Sweep and Bess. They've won on the mainland, too.'

We came abreast of the stone-built fank. I wasn't particularly interested, for my mind was on Rona and on what I was going to say to Sergeant McPhee. But Nappy Neil had slowed down again and was looking curiously from the side-window at the small area of brown earth which the dogs were excavating with excited forepaws.

It was lucky he had slowed down, because all at once he jammed on the brakes, and the station-wagon jerked to a breath-taking halt. I nearly went through the windscreen. In fact my forehead did strike the glass.

'What the hell!' I exclaimed.

Nappy Neil put the engine out of gear, switched it off and opened the door in one swift series of movements.

Then he was out on the road in the buffeting wind, and I was at his heels. I had suddenly seen what he had seen.

The collies were yelping and digging. Old Hector Mathieson – I remembered him now: he had been a tenant with my father, in this same farm of Drumlochan – Old Hector was shambling down the field towards the fank, shouting and cursing. Beneath his sou'-wester, his bearded face was flushed with cold and anger.

Nappy Neil and I vaulted the wire fence and reached the fank before him.

'Sweep! Bess!' he was shouting. 'Come in to my foot! Come in to my foot!'

But they paid no heed. Nor did Nappy Neil and I. We were staring at a man's arm sticking up out of the earth, and as the dogs continued to dig we saw a face appearing.

Old Hector reached us, waving his stick. 'What the hell's gone wrang wi' ye!' he bellowed to his collies. 'Come in to my—'

He stopped abruptly, mouth agape.

The dogs whined as he pulled them off with his bare hands. He struck at them with his crook, and they jumped back. But they remained close to the scene, sitting on their haunches, panting with outstretched tongues and watching avidly.

Carefully I uncovered the face, picking up a soiled

scrap of paper as I did so and absent-mindedly putting it in my pocket. For a moment I didn't recognize the man, for the left side of his head had been shattered by what looked like hail from a shot-gun.

Then Nappy Neil said, *'Harringay!'* – and I knew at last why the fisherman-poet had been away from the hotel for so long.

Audibly swallowing, he added: 'We – we must get the police.'

Eddying round the wall, the wind made a sudden assault on the body. The earth-stained coat-sleeve covering the protruding arm fluttered and shook and dropped back from the brown wrist. This time the ugliness of death had no physical effect on me. All I could feel was a kind of numb horror, which, though it never interfered with the process of thought and action, continued to trouble me throughout the day.

Old Hector wiped a hand across his mouth. 'What has come over us?' he muttered. 'What have we done to deserve it?'

'Wait here,' said Nappy Neil. 'Peter and I will get the police.'

'Very well. But—'

'We'll be back in less than five minutes. It's only half-a-mile to the village.'

He drove fast, skidding to a stop outside the station. In the bar-office we found Sergeant McPhee and Constable Anderson busy with a pile of papers. We told them what the dogs had found.

Sergeant McPhee winced, as if we had struck him. But in a matter of seconds he was himself again, cloaked in severe professionalism.

'Will you run me back to the field in your station-wagon, MacDonald?'

'Ay. Of course.'

'Good. Anderson, get hold of the doctor – if he's not in his surgery he can't be far away – and bring him along in the police car, pronto.'

'Very good, Sergeant.'

'McKechnie!' he shouted, and the second policeman came running from a side room. 'McKechnie, look after the station till we get back.'

'Right, Sergeant. But what—'

'We don't require Mr Parsons. I'd like him to wait here till I come back. He'll tell you what has happened.'

He took a notebook and camera from the desk, then hurried out, trailing Nappy Neil and Constable Anderson behind him. I was glad I didn't have to go back to where the body sprawled in its shallow grave. But I didn't appreciate the inference in what the Sergeant had just said. It seemed that at the best I was under surveillance.

McKechnie would be about forty. Unlike Anderson, who was younger and leaner and sported a small, black moustache, he was stoutly built with a rubicund, clean-shaven face which seemed to mirror good nature. But when the others left and I sat down on a wooden bench against the wall, he made no friendly advances.

All he said was: 'Well, Mr Parsons, what's all the fuss about?'

I told him, omitting none of the grim details.

When I had finished, he sat down stiffly on the high stool at the desk near the window. 'A shot-gun wound, you say?'

'As far as I could make out that's what it was.'

'*Dhia!*' he said. 'This would have to happen just when we're cut off from the mainland!'

People were already moving in the street – men, mostly young men whose curiosity was stronger than their fear. In close groups they walked quickly down the road in the wake of the station-wagon, their coats and trouser-legs flapping in the gale. Seconds later I saw Dr Barbour emerge from his house, hurriedly buttoning on a burberry as he stepped into the waiting police car. The car drove off.

Then from Mrs McIntosh's tall boarding house there burst a group of reporters, led by the bearded Innes MacInnes. Some were in the act of chewing or swallowing, as if they'd been interrupted at a late breakfast. Like hounds on a scent, they, too, made tracks for old Hector Mathieson's field.

The shower-wet street was empty now except for a few whirling scraps of paper and half-a-dozen adventurous hens – staggering, gale-struck hens, doggedly scratching for food in the gutters.

But soon a door opened – a door in the cottage next to the shop. A woman with a drab shawl looked out, and I recognized her as Mrs Campbell, Joanna's mother. She was staring down the street, in the direction the cars had gone.

'That service will be more necessary than ever now,' I said.

'Ay. Pity it takes a tragedy to bring the churches together.' Constable McKechnie's brow furrowed, and he spoke with slow Highland solemnity. After a pause he added: 'Can't you give us any help at all, Mr Parsons?'

'I do have something to tell Sergeant McPhee.'

'Ay. We thought you might have.'

'Why?'

'Strange that you were out so early yesterday morning, your clothes all wet and untidy.'

'Who drew your attention to that?'

'The Sergeant noticed.'

But I knew he was lying. I hadn't met the Sergeant until our return to the village at midday. Somebody – as McKechnie himself might have put it – had been 'laying an information'.

Mrs Campbell wiped her eyes with a handkerchief, then wrapped the shawl more closely about herself and went inside again. A young housewife hurried towards the shop, glancing about in a frightened way. A flowered apron fluttered beneath her open mackintosh. As she passed Mrs Campbell's door she made the sign of the cross.

An elderly man, clasping the hand of a little girl, paid a visit to the Post Office. Three boys emerged from a house near the doctor's and ran quickly to the shop. After a minute they reappeared, quarrelling over a carton of boiled sweets. Obviously Murdo Cameron had decided to keep the school closed.

The boys stopped to wrestle and scuffle. A teenage girl wearing tartan jeans – who was probably their elder sister – came running to shoo them home. Nobody was taking any risks.

I said: 'Tell me, Constable – what was the final result of Dr Barbour's post mortem on Terry Jackson? Was he in fact killed before Joanna Campbell?'

Momentarily he glowered at me, as if suspecting a trap. Then he shrugged, probably fortified by the knowledge that in the present circumstances I couldn't escape even if I wanted to.

'Dr Barbour is sure about it now,' he told me.

'Jackson was killed approximately four hours before Joanna Campbell.'

'Four hours, eh?'

'Approximately I said. An hour less – or an hour more: it's impossible to tell to a minute.'

'I see.'

'But the doctor discovered something else, Mr Parsons.'

'Yes?'

'Jackson was lame when he was murdered. The warders say he was perfectly all right before – before he disappeared, so he must have sprained his left ankle jumping down from the prison wall.'

'I remember,' I said. 'I remember seeing the bandage – last night in the mine.'

Once more we lapsed into silence. I continued to think of Rona. She was a star keeping me on course.

Another shower blustered down the street, blurring the window. McKechnie, clearly no expert on small talk, was proving a dismal companion. I set myself to consider the situation – the first time I had tried to make a calm and impersonal survey of the Kersivay killings.

Following Rona's advice, I ignored my own feelings and stood outside, looking inwards.

The rain on the window helped to concentrate my thoughts. I became a producer again, endeavouring to put sense into seeming nonsense, to bring clarity to confusion. In a mass of apparently intractable material I sought a pattern and a purpose.

The Laughing Cavalier had taught me to pick out a common denominator – a character or a basic factor which would be the linking element in the finished production. Here such a character was immediately to hand – the unknown killer, the man who had murdered three people and might murder more if he deemed it necessary.

But who was he? That I couldn't tell. Not yet. The only thing I was certain about now – thanks to Rona – was that it couldn't be me.

Why had he become a killer? Well, this was a simpler question. He had killed Terry Jackson because he had decided that an escaped psychopath would provide the authorities with a ready-made solution to the problem of Joanna Campbell's murder. And now it was beginning to appear as if he had murdered Kenneth Harringay because the fisherman-poet had discovered the reason for Joanna Campbell's death.

The reason for Joanna Campbell's death. Here was the crux. Here was the basic factor – and I hadn't a clue about it.

Or had I? Wait. Those words shrieked into the fog as I battled with my headache near the seaweed factory. Could they be fitted into the pattern?

'... blackmail ... nasty ... barman ...'

Blackmail? Had I stumbled on something? Easy, Parsons, easy!

What about the diamond brooch that Harringay had found in Joanna Campbell's jewel box? Nappy Neil had said it was worth a hundred pounds. Could it have a connexion? Blackmail and diamond brooches often went together. The wages of sin. And the wages of sin is death.

I pulled myself together. Watch the streaming rain. Listen to the howl of the wind. Concentrate, man, concentrate.

Was a pattern beginning to form? Could be. Yes –

a vague kind of pattern, but a pattern all the same. Joanna Campbell – no prude, no saint, a girl in her late twenties, ripe for pleasure. '*Lovers she had and many, for the loves of the world are free.*' Lovers she had and many. Yes, but on her own confession to Mrs MacLeod, in the end she had only one. A special one. A lover with whom she had arranged a meeting on the night of her death. A lover who could afford to present her with a magnificent brooch in return for her embraces, but who could not afford to have her reveal his identity.

'*Blackmail*' – a possible clue. But what about '*nasty*' and '*barman*'? I didn't even try to make guesses. Perhaps I didn't dare to.

Now then, Parsons, change direction. Go back to basic principles – as Rona and the Laughing Cavalier would certainly advise. Consider the character of this murderer.

Very well. He's scheming, arrogant, brutal, indifferent to the sanctity of human life. As his plan begins to go awry, doesn't there appear a hint of desperation, a brittleness, a tendency to break down under strain and lash out like a cornered beast, like Hitler retreating to his bunker? Recourse to a gun – a shot-gun dealing hurried, messy death as compared with the coldly efficient use of a club or a stick – certainly gives that impression.

Is a picture emerging – a picture of someone I recognize?

Unfortunately, no.

A thought occurred. Was I standing too close to somebody to discern the truth? Were my ideas about him based on boyish impressions rather than on present realities? In certain circumstances a man's character may alter radically in twenty years. Those lines of Byron – what were they? Wait a minute. *'And after all, what is a lie? 'Tis but the truth in masquerade.'*

This was it. A masquerader. A chameleon taking on the colour of a twig.

Hold it now. There's another question – a side-issue, it's true, but a side-issue which may help to unravel a more important problem. Who is Harringay? Or rather – who was Harringay?

He was the broadcasting favourite, of course – the popular fisherman-poet. But mightn't he have had another job – a secret job, a job providing a solid income to augment the meagre earnings of a poet? He had quizzed me in an oddly professional way about my cigarette-case. It also seemed probable that he was the 'layer of information' about my dishevelled condition the previous morning.

A plain-clothes policeman? Unlikely. A private eye? Possibly, though no hint of this had ever leaked out in London.

An agent for MI5?

Now, look – don't be melodramatic, Parsons!

But then – come to think about it, the whole situation is melodramatic. The murders in themselves are melodramatic, because, as Rona said, they are out of character – in Kersivay.

My essay in the technique of production threatened to peter out.

There was still confusion, still a mass of undigested detail; and though a few vague items had fallen into place, I had reluctantly to admit that my script was bound to fail unless I discovered an answer to the sixty-four thousand dollar question – 'Who killed Joanna Campbell – and why?'

But that was the answer everyone was seeking. What could *I* do about it?

Suddenly – and disturbingly – I was aware that as a producer I *could* do something. A producer is exposed and vulnerable. He has to take the risks, in order to provide the actors with the glory. It was at this moment, I think, that the seeds of a plan took root and began to grow.

I fumbled in my pocket for a cigarette. My fingers touched the scrap of paper I had picked up near Harringay's body. It was a mere fragment, an inch-square corner torn from a larger piece.

Casually, when McKechnie's attention was caught by a movement in the street, I took it out and glanced at it. One side was blank and grimed with earth. On the other, in the same neat handwriting I'd seen Harringay use in the hotel register, there appeared one word:

'. . . *Nazi.*'

11

'Be Wary How Ye Judge'

WHAT had attracted Constable McKechnie's attention was the quick approach from the street of Murdo Cameron. I returned the paper to my pocket.

The schoolmaster was wearing an old cloth cap and a rubber coat belted at the waist. In one hand he carried a stick with a sheep's-horn handle. He came surging in, bringing part of the gale with him. His eyes had a gleam that in the old days would have meant a hiding for somebody.

'Is it true what my housekeeper has been telling me? About Harringay—' He saw me and stopped short. 'Peter!' he said, almost with alarm. 'What are you doing here?'

I told him.

'Man, poor old Harringay!' He leant on the counter, hands to his forehead, and I was afraid that he'd start to cry. Presently, however, he straightened up. 'Look, McKechnie,' he said, thickly, 'when are you going to make an arrest?'

'That is not for me to say.'

'What about the C.I.D.? Still sitting on their backsides in Glasgow?'

'The storm, Mr Cameron. No steamer, no plane – not for another twenty-four hours.'

'But this is a matter of life and death! Twenty-four

hours – with a killer on the loose! What about a lifeboat – a helicopter?'

'I don't know—'

'Too damned right you don't know! Put yourself in the place of the women and children. Another night in the dark. Another night when every rattle on the door could mean a visit from the murderer—'

'Now, now, there is no need for exaggeration.'

'Exaggeration? My God!' He braced himself. 'Sorry, McKechnie – nothing personal,' he said, more temperately. 'But we've got to do something. See here, I came to ask if I may use your phone. Mine's out of order. So is the one in the kiosk.'

'Out of order?' McKechnie looked surprised.

The schoolmaster's control again betrayed its brittleness. 'Out of order, I said. I tried them. I want to get in touch with the mainland – with the Chief Constable, in fact. We were at University together. In the Army, too. I think I could persuade him to requisition a helicopter.' He broke off. 'Let me use your phone, will you?' he said, and I noticed that his hands were shaking.

'Very well, Mr Cameron. But—'

'I'll be responsible. I'll pay.'

The phone was on the counter. He snatched up the receiver and dialled. Slowly, as he listened, incredulity and then anger appeared in his expression.

He dialled again. Seconds passed. Then he cradled the receiver and left it there.

'All the lines must be out of order,' he said. 'Now we're entirely cut off. Now we're on our own.'

It could have been the way he put it, or perhaps the look in his eyes. Anyway, I shivered.

McKechnie took a turn at jiggling the receiver. The result was still silence.

He scratched his head. 'It was all right half-an-hour ago. Maybe a tree down at Unival terminus. It happened once before – last winter, when there wasn't a phone working in the island for three whole days.'

A slate fell from a nearby roof and burst into fragments on the pavement. Then the orchestration of the storm was disturbed by the sound of approaching cars.

I asked McKechnie if we might smoke. He gave permission. I lit a cigarette for Murdo and one for myself.

When the cars stopped at Dr Barbour's place I didn't look out. There was nothing new to see. I had witnessed the whole performance before. I smoked and kept my mind on Rona. The schoolmaster leant against the counter, waiting.

He hadn't long to wait. Sergeant McPhee and Constable Anderson came in, blowing on their blue, earth-stained fingers. Murdo began to ask questions, but the Sergeant cut him short.

'You will hear all about it at the inquiry, Mr Cameron. Meantime, I have a great deal to do. First of all, I'd like a word with Mr Parsons here.'

The schoolmaster went away. Divesting himself of notebook and camera, McPhee conducted me into the side-room and closed the door.

He sat down heavily at a small desk and waved me to a chair. From an envelope he produced my cigarette case.

'This was found on the corpse,' he said.

'I know.' I drew in a lungful of smoke, slightly puzzled by his air of indifference. 'Sergeant, there's something I must explain. I'm sorry I didn't tell you about it before, but the truth is I was afraid I might incriminate myself. However,' I said, with awful banality, 'better late than never.'

He nodded.

I gave him the facts, including all that Rona had said about my headaches.

He questioned me closely about the screams I'd heard and about the words that had come to me through the fog.

' "Nasty" and "barman" – are you sure these were the exact expressions?'

'I think so. Though admittedly my mind wasn't crystal clear at that particular moment.'

Finally I took the scrap of paper from my pocket and handed it over. I was still puzzled by the change in his attitude. Before his departure to the scene of Harringay's murder, he had regarded me with obvious suspicion. Now he appeared to have lost interest.

But he was interested in the paper. He found an envelope in a drawer and put it inside.

'Yes,' he said, slowly, 'this could fit in.'

'How d'you mean?'

He looked me straight in the eye and for the first time I found myself liking him. His response to my question, however, was oblique.

He said: 'You might as well know that I believe every word you have told me, Mr Parsons. It's possible you could have killed Joanna Campbell – if you did happen to be a psychopath, which I never could believe – but for the other two murders you have perfect alibis.'

I said nothing.

He continued: 'Jackson was killed about eight o'clock the night before last. At that time you were in the hotel bar, drinking.'

'Right.'

'Dr Barbour says that Harringay met his death between three and five o'clock yesterday afternoon. At that time, according to Miss Carmichael, you were in the hotel.'

'You – you checked on that?'

He sighed. 'I have checked on everything I can think of, but – but—'

He wiped a big hand over his face, leaving a dirty mark beside his chin. I felt sympathy for him. Admiration, too. He was more accustomed to administering sheep-dip regulations than to dealing with monstrous problems in murder. But he faced the task without complaint, determined to pursue it as thoroughly as he knew how.

'But never mind my worries.' He tapped the envelope. 'As I said, this could fit in.'

'I don't understand.'

'I'll tell you in confidence, Mr Parsons – Harringay was an agent of MI5.'

So my instinct had been right after all.

'I received official information about him shortly before he arrived in Kersivay during the summer. I wasn't told the purpose of his visit, but my instructions were to provide assistance if he asked for it. As it turned out, he never even spoke to me, either during his first visit or on this second occasion.' He paused, looking down at the desk and slowly rubbing his chin. 'I came to the conclusion, Mr Parsons, that his job was to locate some kind of foreign influence in this island.'

'I see.'

'I have a notion, too, that he found what he was looking for. It's a pity he didn't tell me about it. Had he done so, he might still be alive today.'

'You'll have heard about Joanna's brooch?'

'Oh, yes. From her mother. Mrs Campbell also told me that Harringay referred to it as an important piece of evidence. But I have examined it in the Bank, and as far as I am concerned it is just another diamond brooch. Though of course an expert jeweller might be able to trace its origin.'

'And you can't get it to an expert jeweller until the storm dies down.'

'That is the kind of thing we are up against, Mr Parsons – all along the line.'

Faintly, borne on the wind, there came to us the chiming of the clock on the village hall.

'Quarter to twelve,' said the Sergeant, rising stiffly. 'You will be going to the service?'

'Yes.' I prepared to leave. 'I hope I may be able to help you – later on this afternoon, perhaps.'

He gave me a quick look. 'If you have any further information—'

'There is nothing else I can say,' I told him. 'However, there may be something I can do.'

'I should advise caution.' He measured his words. 'I believe we are dealing with a murderer far more violent and dangerous than Jackson ever was.'

I went outside and made my way against the wind towards the hall. Other people were moving in the same direction. The hens were suddenly outnumbered by humans.

At the door I found Nappy Neil, waiting for me.

'Did you tell McPhee?'

'Yes. He doesn't suspect me any more.'

'Good for you, Peter! Nothing ever turns out as badly as you imagine, does it?'

As we went in I said: 'Did the police find Harringay's fishing-rod?'

He looked puzzled. 'Not with the body. Should they have?'

'He had one with him when he left the hotel yesterday afternoon.'

'I see. Though his body was buried in old Hector's field, you think he was killed somewhere else?'

'Last night in the hotel, just before I went to sleep, I heard a car on the road. About half-past one it would be.'

'Have you told McPhee about this?'

'Not yet. It didn't occur to me until now.'

Already the place was fairly full, but we had no difficulty in finding seats at the back. I was conscious of a continuous murmur of hushed voices, scraping chairs, whining wind; of a smell of old varnish mingling with that of damp rubber coats.

Most of the villagers were there; and, judging from the line of cars outside, many had come from outlying parts as well.

Near the front I saw Murdo Cameron and Major Rivington-Keel talking to the silver-haired Governor of the prison. Behind them were several tough-looking young men whom I took to be medical orderlies, because amongst their number I spotted my companion of the search-party, Alec Thomson.

In a still, black-garbed group opposite a side-entrance sat Arabella McCuish and other relatives of Joanna Campbell. As we waited they were joined by Maggie McLeod, in tears, and a poker-faced

Roderick Dhu. But old Annie Mary wasn't there. Nor was Joanna's mother. They remained at home, each with sad thoughts for company.

Then the King and his grand-daughter, followed by Katie McCuish and Fiona Kennedy, moved slowly down the passage and took their places. The King was a frowning giant, nodding absently to his friends. Rona was very pale, but straight-backed in her dark suit. I wondered what she was thinking about.

Nappy Neil said: 'They've come in Miss Rona's Anglia. After he'd seen Harringay's body, McPhee made me drive him to the hotel, so that he could ask questions about you. Miss Rona had all the answers.' He smiled, then added: 'Mr Ross said he had no objection to the station-wagon being used by the police.'

The reporters arrived, talking loudly and making a considerable disturbance; but the atmosphere in the hall had a sobering effect, and almost at once, directed by Innes MacInnes, they slipped quietly into seats behind us.

I heard them whispering amongst themselves, excited and disturbed not only by the new sensation of Harringay's death but also by the discovery that their means of communication with the mainland had broken down.

'Talk about eyeless in Gaza. We're tongueless in Kersivay!'

'What about carrier pigeons?'

'Be your age, John! Pigeons fly only one way. Home.'

'My paper,' announced Innes MacInnes, 'will soon

catch on. I shall be surprised if they don't charter a helicopter.'

'Or perchance the *Queen Mary.*'

'But – but for God's sake, what about the rest of us?'

'We'll take care of your stuff – for a consideration.'

'I thought consideration and the *Gazette* were mutually exclusive.'

'Exclusive, Willie? Surely a new word in your vocabulary?'

'Ach, to hell with you!'

'Look – never mind the technical stuff. Will somebody tell me if this Harringay is the wireless bloke?'

'He *was* the wireless bloke. The fisherman-poet. The pin-up boy of Woman's Hour.'

'How the heck does he come into it?'

'We're on to the story of the year,' said Innes MacInnes. 'If not of the century. I have a feeling. Apart from the traditional ingredients – murder, sex, money, and now religion – there's something else. The hidden evil. The canker in the apple. I know these islands. As a rule they're warm-hearted, plain living, plain thinking. But here in Kersivay it's different. There's an influence – a foreign influence. Tension in the wrong places. If I'm not mistaken there's some pretty high-powered bluff going on.'

'D'you mean spies?'

'Pray for guidance, John. Spies are old hat nowadays. They don't even rate a by-line.'

'Then what the hell are you nattering about?'

'I don't know. I have a feeling.'

I had a feeling, too. I lost interest in the talk of the newspapermen and looked around the hall.

I saw farmers in uncomfortable stiff collars; farm-labourers in thin, cheap suits; shepherds with their dogs in the passage beside them; housewives with head-squares; one or two older children; off-duty coastguards in uniform; blue guernseyed fishermen from the port beyond Unival; an airport official; Lachie Robertson from the garage, unembarrassed in greasy overalls. And now, standing solidly at the door, hands behind his back as he took stock of the congregation, I saw Sergeant Donald McPhee.

McKechnie and Anderson were absent. So was Dr Barbour.

I had a feeling. Was the murderer hiding under the common cloak of sorrow and devotion? At that moment my answer would have been in the affirmative. But I would have been interested to know the mind of Sergeant McPhee.

As it approached twelve o'clock, the hall grew quieter. Then a slight noise occurred at the back. I looked round. A blonde teenage girl with crutches was being helped to a seat by the hall-keeper.

'Chrissie Paterson,' explained Nappy Neil. 'The postmaster's daughter. She's had polio.'

But I scarcely heard him. I wasn't even thinking about the girl. Knowledge had begun to nag in my mind. Knowledge that the murderer had given himself away – that if only I could remember something, that if only I could remember and relate two factors, my production script would be well on the way to completion.

Somebody had said it. I knew that. Somebody had said it. But the whole thing was a will-o'-the-wisp, as intangible as a dream.

There was a discrepancy. The knowledge nagged and continued to nag. Think back, Parsons. Somebody made a statement – a statement only the murderer could possibly have made. Think back. Pin it down. Oh, man – why should my brain go woolgathering? Murdo Cameron was speaking, in school, twenty years ago: 'This so-called essay, Parsons. There is only one word to describe it. Woolly, my boy. Woollier than wool!'

The congregation stirred. From a side-door two men walked to the platform and stood together at a wooden table. Both wore clericals. One was small and stout, with apple-red cheeks. His companion was tall, his face lined and thin.

'You wouldn't think it,' said Nappy Neil, 'but the wee fat one is the Reverend Archibald Currie of the Church of Scotland. The other is Father Rafferty.'

Even the physical aspect of the clerics was unexpected: a reverse of the popular concept, a comment on Kersivay's tragedy. Nothing was what it seemed. Mr Hyde masqueraded as Dr Jekyll. A chameleon sat on a twig, brilliantly camouflaged. If only I could remember. If only I could isolate the discrepancy. If only—

But the Rev. Archibald Currie had begun to pray. I gave my mind to the act of worship.

It was a heartening service, not only because Protestants and Roman Catholics were united to plead deliverance from evil, but also because the men of religion kept their words as simple as the words of the Bible. *For now we see through a glass, darkly; but then face to face; now I know in part; but then shall I know even as also I am known. And now abideth faith, hope, charity, these three; but the greatest of these is charity.*

Fr. Rafferty prayed for the soul of Joanna and for

comfort for her friends. The minister spoke of Terry Jackson and Kenneth Harringay, both dead in a strange island, with no relative to mourn for them. 'But this day we of Kersivay take the place of their dear ones and bear their grief. *"O mortal men! Be wary how ye judge. Here pity most doth show herself alive when she is dead"*.'

I saw that Rona's shoulders were trembling. I loved her and wanted to be with her.

At the end an old man with a grey beard and a lovely tenor voice stood up to lead the singing of a psalm – the 23rd Psalm, to the tune of Crimond.

'He makes me down to lie in pastures green: he leadeth me the quiet waters by.' Faltering at first, the voices rose and finally overcame the dull thunder of the gale.

Behind us, caught in the spell, reporters sang in an earnest mumble of bass; for in spite of his surface sophistication, no one responds more warmly to human tragedy than a newspaperman. As verse succeeded verse, however, it wasn't to strangers that I listened but to the folk of Kersivay.

The wail of the sopranos, the lingering harmony of the tenors – these were essentially Hebridean. A lump came to my throat; a kind of nostalgia took hold of my spirit. This was my island, my people. I could sing as they sang, if I had a mind to. *'Goodness and mercy all my life shall surely follow me.'*

Mercy?

In Rona – and in Kersivay – I had found mercy. It was my duty to show gratitude. Before the day was done and darkness fell – no matter what the cost to myself, no matter what terrible secret might emerge

– I was determined to face the murderer and put an end to the terror of his crimes.

And now, as the congregation rose after the Benediction and began to file out, I knew exactly how I was going to do it.

12

Holy Joe's Howff

NOBODY lingered outside the hall for long. The wind was still gusting, with a foretaste in it of the bite of winter.

Nappy Neil said: 'I'm going to collect some stuff at the shop. The station-wagon's there. I'll not be a minute if you'd like to wait.'

'Right. I'll wait,' I called after him.

Rona came across, walking firmly in high-heeled shoes.

In a low voice she said: 'What happened, Peter – at the police station?'

'I'm in the clear.'

'Oh, darling, how wonderful!' Her smile came, doing crazy things to my heart as usual. 'Forgive me now,' she went on, 'but Granpa and I have to hurry back with Katie and Fiona for the lunches. In spite of everything, we can't keep Mr Catford waiting! See you soon.'

'I hope so,' I said; but I wasn't sure.

As I watched them leave in the pale blue Anglia, I heard voices behind me. They belonged to Murdo Cameron and Major Rivington-Keel. They were doing the stiff upper-lip act, though it was evident that both were deeply affected, emotionally.

'Roderick Dhu and Maggie want to spend some

time in the village,' said the laird, carefully, 'so I'm lunching at the hotel and picking them up later. Meantime, Murdo and I are rooting out the doc and taking him for a drink. Badly in need of it, all of us. We'd also like a word with the King. Care to join us? I can give you a lift.'

'Ay, come on,' the schoolmaster put in. 'Do you good, boy. You look like the ghost of *Gleann nan Taibhis*!'

'Thanks a lot, but I have one or two things to do. I'll get back with Nappy Neil,' I said.

'Ah, well – pity!' The Major frowned, coughed, then brought to the surface the thing that troubled him. 'Hell of a business, Parsons – this about Harringay!'

I nodded.

Loudly, above the noise of the wind, Murdo said: 'Look, Major – you knew him as well as any of us. Shooting, fishing, mucking about generally on the estate. Was there anything—'

'No, dammit, nothing! Been thinking, all through the service. Good chap. Knew how to handle a rod – say that for him. Been asking myself, who the hell would want to kill Harringay?'

He mumbled to a stop and brushed his moustache with the thumb and forefinger of his right hand.

As if reluctantly, he added: 'There's just one thing.'

'Go on, man.'

'Interested in Joanna. Never thought much about it until now. Hot little bitch, Joanna.'

The schoolmaster's face grew red. 'How do you mean – interested?'

'Well, talking about her. Saw them together in the glen one night. May have fancied a nibble. Don't blame him.'

Murdo's grip tightened on the handle of his stick. I knew what he was thinking. Insensitive army type. Compares a 'nibble' to a natural function. Would perform with a Zulu if the opportunity arose – and forget about it in five minutes. Incapable of appreciating that a man like Harringay would look for someone with more to offer than physical assets.

He said: 'I refuse to believe it, Major!'

Rivington-Keel shrugged. 'Oh, well – *de mortuis*, I suppose. May have misjudged him. Anyway, always fond of the chap. Dammit, where's all this going to end?'

'That's what I'd like to know. Come on,' growled the schoolmaster. 'I need that drink.'

They started off down the street, leaning back against the gale. The Major's car was parked at the doctor's. They rang his doorbell and went inside.

I found Nappy Neil at the shop, loading groceries into the station-wagon. The plan in my head was beginning to take definite shape.

I said: 'Look, I want to talk to you, somewhere out of this damned wind. Any place in the village where we can get a quiet drink – and something to eat?'

'What's wrong with the hotel?'

'I'm not going back there. Not just now. Not till I get something straightened out.'

'Feeling all right, Peter?'

'If you mean by that have I a headache coming on, the answer is no.'

He said nothing for a second; but finally he appeared to make up his mind. 'There's Holy Joe's howff – down yonder behind the chapel. A bit primitive, but—'

'Suits me. When will you be ready?'

'Give me two minutes. Would you like to go in and see Arabella and old Annie Mary?'

I shook my head. 'I don't want to see anybody. Just you, Nappy Neil. Can I give you a hand with the groceries?'

'No, thanks. I'm about finished.'

As he carried a number of parcels into the back of the station-wagon I stood at the pavement-edge, balancing in the wind. I was beginning to feel cold. Or perhaps not cold exactly. The quivering in my muscles might have been caused by simple fear. For now I realized that my plan would require considerable courage, and courage wasn't my strongest characteristic.

I saw Sergeant McPhee climb into the police car and drive off in the direction of the hotel. The hall-keeper passed me on his way home, lifting a finger to his cap. Lace curtains in the houses opposite were inched to one side. People were watching me. In the old days their troubles had often been resolved by a Parsons. Was a latter-day Parsons capable of doing the same?

I shivered and longed for a drink.

At last Nappy Neil shut and locked the double doors. 'All set,' he said.

We walked down the street, dodging puddles. 'Annie Mary was asking for you,' he went on. 'She's in one of her queer moods today. Seems to think you've come specially to put things right in Kersivay. "Mister Peter knows," she kept on saying. "Mister Peter knows who it is." I expect she was just havering.'

'Yes. I don't know who it is. Though I mean to find out.'

He sighed. 'She has the second sight. Or so they say.'

'Well, she may not be completely wrong. I believe I do know who it is – subconsciously. There's something – something nagging at the back of my mind. A slip-up. A statement of fact which only the killer could have made.'

'Can I help?'

'I don't think so. Either it comes to me or not. My plan doesn't depend on it coming.'

'Plan? What on earth are you talking about?'

Holy Joe's had a tatty, swinging sign:

JOSEPH O'BROLLOCHAN — CAFÉ AND GENERAL STORE.

Nappy Neil led me through a dim little shop smelling of soap and cinnamon balls into an even dimmer apartment at the back. There were no windows. A few empty tables stood in the middle of the linoleum-covered floor, surrounded by piles of cheeses and empty potato-bags.

The bags gave off a strong smell of dry earth; but a coal fire burned in the grate and the room seemed warm and comfortable enough after the chill outside. The sounds of the gale were completely cut off.

Nappy Neil opened a side door and shouted through: 'Are you there, Joe?'

As we sat down at one of the tables a big bald man came waddling in. His eyes were slits in a vast pale face. Rolls of fat hung over the tight polo-neck of his red sweater. Round a wobbling, protruding stomach was tied a striped apron which flapped about his thin legs.

He switched on a naked bulb and came forward, wheezing. 'Och, 'tis yourself now, Nappy Neil!' His accent was Highland out of West Country Irish. 'When at all did we last have the pleasure of your company?'

Nappy Neil ignored the question. 'This is Peter Parsons,' he said, quickly. 'You'll have heard of the Parsons, who used to be in the Big House?'

'Sure, sure.' He held his hand out, and I shook what felt like a bunch of link sausages. ''Tis an honour to make your acquaintance, Mr Parsons.' Then, absently wiping the oilcloth on our table with his apron, he shook his head, apparently on the verge of tears. 'A sad, sad time you have chosen to visit us, indeed! Poor Joanna now – many's the time she sat in here, drowning her sorrows.'

'Had she sorrows, Mr O'Brollochan?'

'Nappy Neil will tell you.' He sighed gustily, but his eyes narrowed even more. 'A great howff this used to be for the young folk of the village – until our trouble came on us two days ago. And Joanna one of my best customers. A high-stepper in her day, Mr Parsons; but och, this last wee while her sparkle had gone. Hard and silent she was, as if troubled.' He heaved another sigh, coughed, lowered his voice and said: 'Now, gentlemen, what can I be doing for you?'

'We'd like half a dozen of your salt beef sandwiches,' said Nappy Neil. 'With a pot of good strong tea. And something to warm us up, maybe.'

'Sure, boy, sure. Anything to oblige.'

While he was away, Nappy Neil told me about this strange character. I was glad to listen and forget for a while what I had to do.

During the war Private O'Brollochan, J., had been cook with an infantry training unit stationed on the island. In later years he came back, married a barren widow with whom he had been billeted and settled down to conduct this small shop and café. But his wife had died; he had been left alone, and his predilection for intrigue – for its own sake rather than in hope of any resultant profit – had given his business a questionable reputation. He had no licence to sell spirits; but a drink could be had from him if you wanted it. He plied you with drink as his guest, and charged high prices for salt beef sandwiches and tea. The folk of Kersivay called him Holy Joe in much the same way as the ancient Greeks used to call the Furies *Eumenides,* the well-meaning ones; for he knew a great many of the island's secrets and, if roused from lethargy, could be a dangerous enemy.

But on this occasion he wasn't telling secrets. In fact, despite his tortuous hints about Joanna Campbell, I don't think he knew any more about her than did everyone else. When he brought the tea and sandwiches, which were flanked on a tin tray by an unlabelled half bottle of whisky and two tumblers, I tried to question him; but he only growled in his throat and did his best to look wise.

I gave him thirty shillings, which seemed to satisfy him. We had a dram together. Then he wheezed away, hinting at the presence of a mysterious friend in the kitchen, and for a time Nappy Neil and I munched our sandwiches in silence. They were excellent sandwiches, if somewhat coarsely cut, and I was thinking that a hundred years ago Joe O'Brollochan – even in the matter of his outlandish name – might have been perfectly cast as the proprietor of a shebeen.

At last Nappy Neil said: 'This plan of yours, Peter – what's it all about?'

Reluctantly I switched my thoughts to the present. 'I'd like you to do something for me,' I said.

'How come?'

'You'll be going to the hotel soon. I want you to spread a story, first of all in the village – in the shop, the Post Office – then in the hotel. You can tell it in the bar, to Katie in the dining-room.' He was about to say something, but I stopped him. 'The story is that I'm going up into *Gleann nan Taibhis* this afternoon – about five o'clock, three hours from now. I'm going by myself. I'm going because I've found out who the murderer is and because I believe that in the old mine I can lay hands on certain evidence which will convict him.'

His face had gone white. 'But for heaven's sake, Peter – if you know anything—?'

'I don't, Nappy Neil! I keep telling you. But can't you see – if the killer thinks I do, if he's scared of having overlooked some evidence in the mine, if he knows I'm all alone up there in the glen, he may decide to try and kill me. In that case I'll have his number.'

He sighed, thrusting fingers through his sandy hair.

'Peter Parsons – high-class bait. I think you're crazy!'

'Listen. You always ran the show when we were children. Now I'm running this one. We can't afford to wait for the C.I.D. Even though they do arrive tomorrow they may take weeks to discover the truth. They may never discover it. Meanwhile there could be more killings. This is my way of bringing the abscess to a head.'

'I can see the possibilities. At the same time, Peter, you're risking your life—'

'I hope I'll be able to look after myself.'

Clearly he was unconvinced. 'This plan of yours may have something to it – I admit that. But couldn't some of us help? Murdo Cameron and me, for instance. Maybe Willie Ross—'

'That's the last thing I want.'

'But we'd stay out of sight. We'd simply have you under observation, as it were.'

'No, Nappy Neil! You'll keep the truth of this to yourself. Understand?'

He stared at me. He opened his mouth to speak, then thought better of it. Realization of what I had in mind suddenly showed in his eyes.

Finally he grabbed the bottle, poured out a dram and gulped most of it down. 'I get it,' he said, coughing quietly. 'You trust nobody.'

'That's right – with two exceptions. If the plan is to succeed, the killer must be convinced that I'm alone in the glen.'

'You'd never get away with it, Peter!'

'Why not?'

'He'd kill you. How could you defend yourself?'

'I'll tackle that problem when the time comes.'

He struck the table with his fist. 'I refuse to do it! I refuse to spread this damn fool yarn—'

'Nappy Neil! I may be a fool. I may have ideas above my station in life. But this is my native island. This is my home. Kersivay's been good to the Parsons for more than three hundred years. Now I'd like to pay back some of the debt. Or try to.'

He kept looking into my face, his body taut and still. 'You agree with Annie Mary, then?'

'How d'you mean?'

'That evil has come to Kersivay. An evil of arrogance.'

'I think so. Time it was rooted out.'

'Why pick on me to lend a hand?'

'Because you're one of the two people I trust.'

He leant forward. 'Are you sure?'

'Absolutely. We were friends at school. We're friends now. The twenty years in between count for nothing.'

'I used to be the boss. Now you've taken over.'

'For this production only.'

'I see.' He lowered his eyes, tracing the pattern in the oilcloth with a finger. 'I'll tell you something, Peter. Remember you asked Holy Joe if Joanna had sorrows and he said, "Nappy Neil will tell you"?'

'I remember.'

'Well, she had sorrows all right. I was one of them.' He looked up, and I saw strain and even guilt in his expression. 'At any rate I was one of those who took what she had to offer and gave nothing in return.'

'Maybe that's the way she wanted it.'

'I thought so at the time, but now I'm not so sure. I believe that all her life she was looking for someone she could love – someone who in return would give her security.'

For a time there was silence.

Then I said: 'Does Katie know?'

'Ay. One day I began to tell her, but she stopped me and said she'd heard all about it.' He drank what remained of the whisky in his glass and went on: 'Joanna used to come and see me in the hotel – in the annexe, at night. I sleep there alone, you see, so it was convenient. But of course as soon as I began to go steady with Katie I dropped her like a hot brick. Talk about arrogance!'

'We're none of us saints, Nappy Neil.'

'I know. But some of us get a better deal than others.' He got up suddenly, and the bottle and the tumblers rattled on the tin tray. 'After that, do you still trust me?'

'More than ever.' I got up too.

'Even if I tell you that Joanna never allowed Katie to forget what had happened – that she'd laugh in our faces when she met us on the road together?'

I nodded. 'What you've told me makes no difference. Now then, will you spread the story?'

He hesitated. The room was quiet, except for the hiss of a gas-filled coal in the grate. Then the strain left his eyes and he managed a crooked smile.

'All right, I'll do it. Maybe you can look after yourself better than I thought. Anyway, the MacDonalds were aye sib to the Parsons.'

In a less prosaic era we might have shaken hands. Instead we simply nodded to each other.

'You'll be staying here for a while?' he said.

'Until about four o'clock. Then I'll make tracks for the glen.'

At the door he turned. 'You said there were two of us. I think I know who the other one is.'

Then he was gone. I sat down, alone in Holy Joe's, and had another dram.

I badly needed it.

13

Bait for a Killer

THE fire burned low, and I began to feel the cold again.

At about three o'clock, Holy Joe reappeared. If he was surprised to find me still there he didn't show it.

'Well, well now, Mr Parsons, 'tis real thoughtless I am!' He heaved himself across to an iron bucket of coal and worked at replenishing the fire. 'But I had business with a friend of mine – important business.' He jerked a thumb in the direction of the kitchen and assumed an expression both knowing and mysterious.

Then he stood up, wiping his hands on his apron, and leered at the empty half bottle. 'Would you be caring for another, maybe? On a cold day like this and after all the excitement—'

'Yes,' I said. 'Bring me another, please.'

'Sure, sure. Man, 'tis proud I am to serve one of the real gentry. One of the old stock. Just you wait now – I'll not be a jiffy.'

On his return I got the idea that he was all set for a comfortable chat. But I didn't encourage him. I wanted a drink. I wanted to be alone with my problem during the next long hour.

At any other time I might have been interested in his gossip. In the circumstances, however, I found it difficult even to grasp what he was saying. All my energies were concentrated on the programme ahead of me.

I poured him out two substantial drams and, while he absorbed them in a lengthy lip-smacking routine, did my best to be sociable; but at last, obviously disappointed in my taciturnity, he went away. The ensuing silence – and yet another drink – brought me a spurious sensation of mental clarity.

Nappy Neil had been right. I was a fool. A vainglorious fool, making a gesture which could only be described as stupidly sentimental and dangerous.

I began to suspect even my own motives. Was I, in fact, taking a risk for the benefit of Kersivay, as I had boasted, or merely for the benefit of my own ego? Was my desire to unmask the killer aroused by a sense of public responsibility, or did it really stem from a hope of proving beyond doubt that my black-outs were a normal disability and that I was stronger and braver than I had hitherto appeared to my friends?

I took another mouthful of whisky. Human motives were difficult to analyse – perhaps in this case impossible to analyse. Their name was legion; they were inextricably mixed. Leave it at that, Parsons. Leave it at that and carry on.

The fire seemed warmer, the smell from the potato-bags less unpleasant. I looked at my watch. Three-thirty. In half-an-hour the green light would be on. The sound-mixer's hand would flicker over the panel, and the programme would begin. *'Bait for a Killer'* – written, devised and produced by Peter Parsons. There was only one snag. The ending had still to be improvized. It depended solely on the reaction of the main character – and on the skill of the producer.

What the producer needed was another dram to steady him. He had one.

He felt on top of his job now, fully confident that the programme was going to be a success. He was afraid, of course – but that was only natural. He was afraid of death, if the killer struck without warning. He was afraid of life, if the killer proved to be—

Drop it, Parsons! Drop the speculation. Keep two things clearly in mind – the evil of arrogance and the mark of the beast. Don't think about this man as a friend, or even as a human being. Keep it objective. Let sentiment take a holiday. Let the producer finish the bottle and reject dull care.

I finished the bottle and peered at the face of my wrist-watch. Ten minutes to four. Any time now I could be making a start.

I got up, swaying a little. Parsons, don't say you've made the producer drunk! Drunk at the panel, with a programme almost due – the final sin and ignominy. The seal of incompetence.

I struggled to control my muscles, standing at the fire; but as I lit a cigarette my fingers continued to shake. This condition wasn't the result of incompetence, I argued, but of natural apprehension. A man undergoing strain has a right to fortify himself. A man bound for the scaffold is allowed a drink. Two drinks. Three drinks—

Steady man – steady! You're forgetting Rona. Rona with her dark hair and her comforting arms and the smile that makes your heart happy. Innocent and vulnerable. Trusting you, relying on your will and purpose. *'The Parsons were fine people. Real island people. I was brought up in that belief.'*

I took a deep breath and squared my shoulders. I

loved her. This was it – the basic factor, which until now I had been too blind to see. This was the linking element. The main character would presently emerge from the shadows, and the whole production would become a unity.

Four o'clock. I opened the door and went out through the dim, dark shop into the street. With a small shock of surprise I found that the gale no longer existed. Only a fresh breeze blew from the west, fanning my hot cheeks and making the whisky hum and hiss even more powerfully in my head.

I met two people as I went down the road. A tinker with a sidelong swing, heading for Holy Joe's, and an old woman in a doorway, who crossed herself as I passed. Neither of them spoke. I was glad of silence.

The best way into the glen was through the plantation on Drumlochan. When I reached old Hector Mathieson's field I climbed the fence, pausing for just a second to glance at the mound of earth near the road.

The sheep were gone now. I saw nothing living except a big brown hare which loped off into the wood on the right. It had been squatting near Harringay's temporary grave. I shivered, remembering the superstition about the transference of souls. Had Harringay screamed like a hare when the pellets tore into his face?

The exercise began to sober me. I was wearing a sports jacket and flannels, which would be poor protection if it rained. I wished I had thought in the morning about bringing a mackintosh. But in fact the afternoon was now fairly clear, and the showers had grown less frequent. It was cold, though. Bitterly cold.

The plantation was quiet. My feet sank in piles of fallen leaves. Twigs broke under my shoes like pistol-shots. The trees soared upwards, gaunt and tall, like pillars in a cathedral.

I knew my way. Nappy Neil and I had often played here, quarrelling over our respective roles as cowboy and Red Indian. In the end I had usually been the Red Indian, doomed to bite the dust. Today, I hoped that for once I might play the cowboy.

Presently I got the idea that I was being watched. Tension made me walk stiffly and fast. Once or twice, as I glanced to the right or left, I stumbled on hidden obstacles and almost fell. But there was nothing to see – only crowded vistas of ash and fir and rowan.

A grouse rose from under my feet, cackling off amongst the tree-trunks as if radar-controlled. My heart leapt and pounded. I discovered I was no longer cold. I was sweating. The great producer, the great man intent upon succouring Kersivay, sweating like a nightmare-ridden child.

Call it off, Parsons. Heroics are not for you. Rona will understand. Nappy Neil will understand. The police and C.I.D. men are trained to do this kind of job. They dislike interfering amateurs. Leave it to the professionals, and retire from the lists with honour.

Honour? Man, what a state you're in! It's the drink, of course. The demon drink. Why the hell did you go and make such a fool of yourself in Holy Joe's?

You've got to face the facts. If you call it off now you're a dead duck – finished, caput. Not in a literal sense. You'll go on breathing, but in every other way you'll be dead. You'll hate and despise yourself and guzzle more drink to blur the pain. And drink will encourage more headaches, more black-outs.

Suddenly I found that I had a headache, and the knowledge edged me towards despair. Why should this happen, just when I wanted to be fit and strong and in full command of all my senses? Damn Holy Joe! Damn Nappy Neil—

No, it wasn't Nappy Neil's fault. It was entirely my own. I had looked for Dutch courage and it had turned into a headache.

I came to a little burn, running noisily through the wood down towards the river. It was about ten feet across and deep with flood-water. I had to make a jump.

The banks on either side looked fairly firm, though padded with leaves. In the shadows of my mind the thought persisted that eyes were watching me; but I didn't care. I was past caring about anything, except that I must go on – headache or no headache – and reach the glen.

I went back about twenty feet and sprinted towards the burn. I leaped and landed on the far bank. But one foot must have struck a stone under the leaves, and a quick pain stabbed through my right ankle. I sprawled on my face and slid sideways into the water.

The shock of cold around my thighs brought quick reaction. I scrambled up the bank and knelt, panting, on the leaves. My flannels were soaking wet. My ankle was hurt. But worst of all I felt suddenly and desperately sick.

It could have been the result of unaccustomed exertion – or, more likely of a surfeit of bad whisky. Whatever the reason, I knelt there and threw up violently until my stomach was empty.

When the bout was over I sat back on my heels,

trembling and exhausted. Somewhere in the vicinity a twig cracked as if splintered by a heavy foot. But I paid no particular attention. I crawled back to the bank, lay down and splashed my face. Then, feeling better, I cupped my hands, filled them with water and had a long drink. It had the tang of earth and peat, but it did me good. After a while the pain in my ankle disappeared, and I was able to stand up.

Only then did it occur to me that I had become fully sober and that my headache was gone. I had a feeling of cleanliness and relief, as if a load of grime had been mangled out of me. I was wet from the waist down, I was cold and physically miserable, but I had regained a sense of purpose.

Fishing a handkerchief from my jacket pocket, I wiped my face and hands. There was often a technical crisis at the beginning of a programme. Now that it was over, I could proceed with the main sequences.

I moved on, intensely aware now of the need for caution. My senses were alert. Some confidence had returned, based this time on reason, not on billowing whisky fumes.

At the far end of the plantation I vaulted the fence and began to bear left across a turnip-field into the lower reaches of the glen. I was in the open now.

Scrub-filled, *Gleann nan Taibhis* burrowed sinuously into the hills, and in the distance I caught a glimpse of white from the waterfall. Its borders burgeoned up to heathery moorland, dotted here and there with white-washed crofts and grey farm-steadings. High on the moor – at the end of my eye's journey – was the Big House, white-gabled, swathed in its hedges of dark red fuchsia.

I crossed a long grassy ridge beyond the turnip-field. Up on the hillside I saw a patch of emerald green – the deadly 'wallee' which Nappy Neil and I, as small boys, had been warned so often to avoid. Despite the warning, however, we had approached to within a few feet of it many times, in order to throw heavy stones and watch them sink into the watery mud of an untapped spring. I wondered if by any chance the killer had thought of it as a disposal point for Jackson's body. Perhaps a body would take too long to disappear. The 'wallee' was less than half-a-mile from the road and in full view of passers-by.

I came to the road and walked along it until it turned sharp right to zig-zag up across the moor. Then I climbed a fence of wire-netting – an innovation to keep lambing ewes from straying on to higher and colder ground – and made my way through a tangle of hemlock to the side of the river.

By the water's edge I stopped and had a look at my cigarettes. The packet was wet, but the inner wrappings had protected the cigarettes themselves. I lit one with a damp match which luckily sparkled to life on a stone and took stock of the situation.

Far behind lay the lowland farms, the hotel and the village, with a clear view beyond of the airport and the sea. On either side hazel-covered banks rose upwards for almost two hundred feet. In front were the shadowed depths of the glen.

For the past half-hour I had seen no one. The glen, too, appeared to be deserted. But it would be easy for a watcher to hide in the undergrowth which topped the high banks, and I had a feeling that I wasn't alone. But that was what I had planned for. I had no complaints.

I inhaled a lungful of smoke, took one last look at

the open strath, then turned my back on it and set off along the riverside. I threw the stub of my cigarette into the brown water. It fizzed and sparked and floated away behind me.

Then, high up on the left, I heard what could have been a quiet warning whistle. I used my will power and continued to move on; but without turning my head I looked in the direction of the sound. An owl floated up from a hazel-tree and slowly volplaned out of sight. Someone had disturbed it: that was fairly certain, because owls seldom fly in daylight unless excited by a human presence.

As I went deeper into the glen I kept furtive watch on the top of this left-hand bank. Once or twice I thought I saw movement amongst the bushes; but I couldn't be certain, for the area was some hundreds of yards away, and in shadow.

My nerves were on edge. Here by the river I was in full view – a simple target, a gift to a man with ambush in his mind. But nothing happened. Not yet.

There was no wind in the glen. No sound, either, except for the gentle rush of water. The gorse thickened on the river-bank. Near one of the more massive clumps I recognized the place where Nappy Neil and I had rested the night before.

Presently, as I skirted a green knoll, I came in sight of the waterfall again, now only half-a-mile ahead. This was where they heard the singing – the ghostly singing of the princess who had died.

I stopped to light another cigarette. There was no singing. But as the match spattered and flamed in the tobacco a blackbird rose noisily from a bramble-bush – behind me and high up to the right. I wheeled round, and for a split second I did see someone. A man with a rifle.

Even as I completed the turn he became invisible amongst the bushes. But I had seen him. I had recognized his bulky figure, his checked tweed jacket.

The man up there was the King.

The King of Kersivay.

14

On the Hook

MOVEMENT on the left. On the right a fleeting glimpse of Willie Ross. My ideas were jolted out of perspective. I had been intent on finding one man – one killer. It seemed now that the killer might have an accomplice. Perhaps several.

And slowly and methodically they were closing in

Sometimes a shock sharpens mental reaction. In this case the opposite was true. I became so panic-stricken that my brain turned cloggy. Coherence vanished under oily swirls.

Only one clear thought persisted. With a single adversary I always had a chance. Against a number I was helpless. But at the present stage there could be no turning back. I had to go on. Before the end I might at least learn the truth.

But did I want to learn the truth? Now that I was on the brink of discovery, was brinkmanship the answer? Wouldn't it be better – much better – for my headache to come now? Surely this was the time for it – the time for a black-out. Oblivion in a black-out, and a quick end to the whole programme.

No headache came. When I wanted it no headache came. I puffed quickly at my cigarette and went forward. Cowboys and Red Indians. Once more into the breach, dear Parsons. Once more into the dust.

Leaving Rona behind – that was the sadness of it. Instead of playing out this ghastly charade I should be running back to her, running back to hide in the shelter of her arms. She loved me – and would continue to love me – not because I wore the tinsel trappings of a hero but for myself, with all those warts on my character which out-Cromwelled Cromwell.

But of course the desire was Freudian, strong in me now because I had never been able to run to my mother. It was a revelation of selfishness, and as I recognized this I understood at last why I had come to *Gleann nan Taibhis*. It was because I loved Rona. Because my love for her was stronger than my selfishness. Because at last I was determined to give rather than to take. I wanted to give her Kersivay as she remembered it.

It seemed now that I should be unable to present the gift in person. A pity. *''Tis true 'tis pity; and pity 'tis 'tis true.'*

I slipped on a patch of loose river-gravel and fell on my hands and knees. I got up and veered right behind the knoll. Here was an area of level turf, screened in front by another hillock and less than fifty yards from where the road curved in above it to the verge of the glen. It was an arena – a tiny natural arena; and in its centre I found what looked like discarded props. A Donegal hat decorated with trout-flies and a broken fishing-rod. Their arrangement reminded me of a still-life by Barrington Brown, except that there was congealed blood on the hat and on the scarred and trampled turf where it lay.

So this was where Harringay had struggled and

been killed. After death it was likely that his body had been carried up to a car on the road and later transported for burial to old Hector's field.

Why?

My brain was oily still; but I reckoned that the answer must fit in with the clue already hidden in my subconscious – the clue which so far I had failed to bring to the surface. The discrepancy. The thing someone had said, unaware that it revealed his guilt.

I left the props where they were and walked on. I began to climb the hillock. When I reached the other side the waterfall would be in full view. At every step I was prepared for something to happen. A rifle-shot from either side. Or a shout and an answering whistle – and my adversaries, at last in the open, conducting a pincer-movement to cut me off from the mine.

Something did happen – but not what I expected. I heard a bleating and a sudden patter, and over the brow of the hillock streamed a line of about a dozen cross-bred lambs. I stood and stared. They ran past me down towards the flat turf. As I turned to watch, the leader saw the Donegal hat directly in his path and jumped over it, springing high and stiffly. The others followed his example, leaping and twisting as they raced for the shelter of the clumps of gorse.

So feeble was my process of thought that it took me some time to realize that the lambs must have been startled by something beyond the hillock. I climbed quickly to the top. Coming down the glen with a shotgun on his shoulder was Major Rivington-Keel. His scarred mouth was pursed. He was whistling an unrecognizable tune.

Relief was my first reaction. I wasn't alone any

more. Surely in the presence of a witness they wouldn't dare to stage a killing. Then it occurred to me that inadvertently the Major had put himself in the same dangerous position as I was in myself. If I were booked for death, then – unless the situation altered – so was he. I had a momentary impulse to shout a warning – to turn and run away, so that my pursuers might follow and give him at any rate a chance to escape.

But wait. His gun – his loaded shot-gun – did that not alter the situation? If I joined forces with him now, wouldn't the enemy think twice before attacking – simply because he possessed a means of retaliation? A shot-gun has never been a match for a rifle. Nevertheless, in the close confines of *Gleann nan Taibhis,* where cover was ample, it might still prove effective enough as a deterrent.

He looked up and stopped whistling. At first he seemed not to recognize me. Then his face broke into a crooked smile and he waved a greeting.

I went down the side of the hillock, and we met on a strand of gravel by the river.

'What's this, Parsons? Walking for the good of your health?'

'Something like that.'

'When we got home this afternoon Maggie told me she wanted something for the pot. Always ready to oblige a lady.' He chuckled, though his eyes were watchful. 'Thought I'd have a go for a couple of rabbits. Not many left nowadays. Myxomatosis.'

'Plenty of hares,' I said.

'Certainly. Never touch 'em, though. I mean, never eat 'em. Too coarse.'

Both to the right and to the left I saw a shivering

of gorse, a trembling of hazel-branches. There was a faint whistle, like the call of a mavis.

If I told him what was happening, would he believe me? Would he fall in with my idea of a united front?

I said: 'Are you not scared to go about alone? With this – murderer at large.'

He shrugged and gave me a sidelong look. 'I was going to ask you the same question. At least I have a gun. You have nothing.'

'That's right. Nothing,' I agreed.

'Heard a rumour in the hotel that you know who this chap is. Matter of fact, one of the waitresses said you'd discovered a clue. In the old mine up there.'

This was my chance to explain, to enlist his help. I hesitated. As an old soldier he'd probably become an immediate and enthusiastic ally; but was it fair to involve him in an encounter which might lead to death?

Because I couldn't bear to lose his company, I compromised. 'Sorry,' I said. 'I don't know who the killer is. But I do have an idea that the old mine may provide a clue. I'm going there to have a look. Care to join me?'

'Why not?' He eased the strap of the game-bag on his back. 'Come on. Haven't seen the old mine for years. I'd like to be in at the death, as it were.'

A vague thought suggested itself. If we reached the shelter of the mine we'd have a fair chance of holding our own, for the Major's bag obviously contained a number of cartridges. And if shooting started, the police would be bound to hear and take steps to relieve us.

We followed the course of the river for about a hundred yards, then began to climb. All around us was a strong and slightly acrid perfume – the mingled scents of damp, peaty earth, of flowering heather and of gorse and bracken undergoing autumnal decay.

Everything remained quiet, except for the increasing noise of the waterfall; but my nerves were still tingling. People were watching us. I knew it.

From time to time the Major glanced at me, as if puzzled. Finally he put his curiosity into words.

'Your trousers, Parsons. Soaking wet. Odd that every time we meet out of doors you're in a mess!'

We were on higher ground, approaching the broad ledge which curved in towards the mine. Clouds of spray from the bottom of the fall smoked up beneath us. The roar of the leaping flood-water filled our ears. More was coming down than had been the case the previous night. The mine entrance was almost entirely hidden by a gauzy brown screen which shimmered in the sunlight.

As casually as possible, I said: 'I slipped and fell, jumping across the burn in the Drumlochan plantation.'

'H'm. Lucky you didn't twist an ankle.'

Twist an ankle? It had happened, though the pain had soon gone. But Terry Jackson hadn't been so fortunate, jumping down from the prison wall. I'd seen the bandage on his foot. At the end of his life he must have been limping, lame—

A thunder in my mind obliterated the thunder of the fall. Lame! This was it. This was the discrepancy, the pointer to guilt. *'Spotted a man in the glen this afternoon. Fishing. Thought at first it might be Jackson, then realized this chap was nearly a foot taller. Wasn't lame, either.'*

The man who said that was the killer. At the time he said it only the killer could have known that Jackson had hurt his ankle, for his body was yet to be recovered.

At last I recognized my adversary. He was by my side, leading me towards the mine just as he had led his first unsuspecting victim.

'Major,' I said, surprised by the calmness of my own voice, 'I think we've gone far enough.'

It was obvious now who had distracted the attention of the original search-party from the area of the waterfall. Nor could there be much doubt as to who had informed the police about my dishevelled state on the morning after Joanna Campbell's death. This man was a great believer in 'insurance'.

He stopped and faced me, there on the rocky ledge, with the cauldron of the river a hundred feet below and the sides of the lonely glen swelling up about us. He saw that I knew. His expression of affability dissolved into one of arrogance and sadistic cruelty. Before my eyes he became an alien personality with the bright, hard look of evil.

Nappy Neil had read the signs. *'Have you seen him kill a rabbit? He takes his time before he breaks its neck.'*

Now I realized that he was going to take his time with me.

As we measured each other, the swirls of oil in my brain were washed away. Suspicion of the man's identity began to grow like an obscene flower.

The pieces fitted. Thick speech and a wound in the mouth. The purchase of the Big House soon after the war. Visits to Europe. A brooch 'worth a hundred pounds.' A red weal on the throat of Terry Jackson –

'the mark of the beast'. The scrap of paper I'd found near Harringay's body, with one word staring up out of the grime. Joanna screaming: *' . . . blackmail . . . nasty . . . barman . . .'*

The pieces fitted. Could they possibly present a true picture?

I said: 'Correct me if I'm wrong, Major. You helped Terry Jackson to escape and killed him, because his disappearance would provide a plausible cover-story when you murdered Joanna Campbell. Then Harringay – helped by MI5 – picked up your trail. You killed him yesterday afternoon, here in the glen. You probably concealed his body in the boot of your car – it may have been there when we met you with Innes MacInnes last night; but some time after midnight you buried it as far away from the Big House as possible. I heard the sound of your engine, by the way. I was also near at hand when you took Joanna out on to the moor, killed her with the butt of your gun and threw her body over the cliff. She was your mistress as well as your servant, I take it?'

'I needed a woman.'

'Quite. She was a hot little bitch – your own description. Sometimes she told Roderick Dhu and Maggie that she was going out to meet a boy-friend; but in fact she simply crossed the yard to the Big House. Eventually, however, she made a discovery and began to blackmail you.'

He nodded, still staring. 'One night she surprised me in my bedroom with the safe open and the jewels in full view. For a time I played safe and presented her with a brooch – which Harringay recognized. Then she guessed who I was, and I had to kill her.'

His eyes were cold. There was a stillness about him, a poised preparedness.

'Who are you?' I said.

'Don't you know?'

'Like Jackson, I can guess.'

'Well?'

I had become unaware of my surroundings. Scents and sounds were obliterated. The glen and the waterfall existed only as a painted backdrop. All my energy was concentrated on maintaining the tableau.

'You are a Nazi,' I said, 'living on Nazi loot. You behave like a Nazi, you kill like a Nazi – gun-barrel across the throat, knee in the back. With her dying breath Joanna screamed – *"You Nazi, Bormann!"* '

'Correct,' he said. 'I am Martin Bormann, heir to the Führer.'

'So now we know why Martin Bormann was never found.' Strangely enough, I couldn't even hate him: feeling had died. 'I can guess how it was worked. A Major Rivington-Keel was captured in the fighting near Lübeck, just when you Nazis had almost reached the end of your tether. His likeness to yourself was pointed out, and when it was discovered that he was a bachelor, with no relatives in England, you decided to steal his identity. You acquired his papers, practised forging his signature. With German thoroughness, you had an operation done on your mouth, so that to begin with – before you learned the language thoroughly – there would be a valid reason for your halting, guttural speech. Rivington-Keel was liquidated. You took his place in the concentration camp hospital near Berlin and let the Americans find you. A war hero, wounded in the mouth for your country. Am I right so far?'

'Near enough.'

'You are flown back to England, gradually your speech improves – and in the end you buy this estate in Kersivay. From time to time – as you told me – you go abroad. To Paris, Monte Carlo, occasionally to a little town called Haaltert in Belgium. You're supposed to be on holiday, but in fact your purpose is to collect your share of the negotiable jewellery which the Nazis have salted away in the vaults of so many European banks. I have no doubt you and your friends still dream of a Nazi revival, a resurgence of Aryan might—'

'That will do!'

His ruddy face paled. His poise was suddenly uncertain, and the tableau threatened to disintegrate. He held the gun across his body. I kept watching it with an avid eye.

'I agree,' I said. 'You've reached the end of the road, Bormann.'

As we faced each other on the ledge his back was towards the waterfall and the entrance to the mine. On his right and my left was a sheer drop to the boiling river.

'The end of the road?' he muttered thickly. 'For you – yes. But not for me. I have work to do. Already a great army of men is gathering in the secret barns and cellars of the Reich. I know. I have spoken to them. I have heard them sing our marching-songs. No Jew or decadent democrat can stop us. In five years, ten years – when the West has crumbled under Communist infiltration – then we will rise up and save the world. And I, as Leader, will give the order for victory.'

It was incredible. Incredible until you remembered

that Hitler, too, had lived in a maze of fantasy. In his mountain-top eyrie at Berchtesgaden, while reports accumulated of reverses in Russia, of defeats at Cassino and Anzio, of Allied successes in France, he still saw himself, by the aid of secret weapons and daring combinations of yet untapped resources, dramatically turning the tables on his enemies. Like his Führer – like all those Nazis and Fascists still scattered like diseased seed in the crannies of the earth – Bormann was creating a mental dream-world to compensate for the bitter reality of failure.

Incredible. Even pathetic. But you have to recognize that in a limited way, such men, though pathetic, can still be dangerous. Like now, for instance. Like now – in this small and fateful moment – as Bormann's eyes glint with killer lust and his body tautens and the gun begins to move upwards—

His thumb was on the safety-catch as I leapt for that gun. I felt cold metal in my fingers and tried to wrench it away from him. But he held on firmly, and all I could do was to thrust it high. One of the barrels went off, and a blast of shot and sound seared past my face.

I scarcely noticed. I had to kill him – or I should be killed. These were the simple alternatives. By a miracle I remained alive, still capable of overcoming him: that was what mattered.

We fought in desperate silence. I brought my knee up to strike him in the groin; but he avoided it by lunging sideways. In his turn he kicked out at my ankles. His boot struck, and for a second the pain was excruciating. I lost my grip on the gun, and he pulled it down and back and was clear.

Again I saw the gun coming up. Again I leapt forward. I caught him about the body in a wrestler's hold, smothering the gun against his chest. I butted with my head and felt his teeth jar into my scalp. He grunted and cursed.

But the impetus of my attack was so savage that we both stumbled, sprawling against the inner wall of turf. Momentarily I was on top of him, but he kicked and heaved, and my hands in the small of his back were torn against a sharp sliver of stone. I loosed him and fell to the side, vainly endeavouring to regain balance. In that bleak instant he stood up and swung his gun. Its butt caught me full on the face.

I didn't lose consciousness, but the shock put out the fire of aggression in my heart. I sank to my knees on the extremity of the ledge, with the airy chasm behind me. He towered above, triumphant.

I expected him to shoot – to empty the second barrel into my skull. But he didn't shoot. Maybe he forgot about the remaining live cartridge. Maybe he reckoned that if my body were found in the river, uninjured except for what could be taken as natural bruising, my death would be considered accidental. Whatever the reason, he simply raised the gun, held it high above his head and prepared to smash my life out with the butt.

I was finished. Concentration left me. With clarity I saw the glen, green and shadowed, heard the rush of the waterfall and the crunch of Bormann's boots, smelt the clean, hard scents of autumn.

This was it. This was oblivion. Earth to earth, dust to dust—

A rifle cracked from above the fall. A redness gushed from the bald patch above Bormann's forehead, and he dropped the gun and reeled towards me, spinning like a run-down top. I tried to catch him; but he fell across me and went over the edge, silent, down and down into the river.

I leant on splayed hands, struck by a reaction of utter weariness.

They came round me – Nappy Neil and Murdo Cameron from below the fall, Willie Ross from above it. I got slowly to my feet, eyeing their rifles.

To Nappy Neil I said: 'I warned you to keep out of it, boy, but in spite of that—'

'You daft idiot!' He wiped sweat from his face with a sleeve of his jersey. 'We had to come and look after you.'

'Ay, the plan was good,' said the schoolmaster. 'But dammit, man, you'd never have carried it out on your own! Friends are always a blessing. This time they were a necessity.'

'Who shot him?'

'I did,' said the King of Kersivay, bulking large above us. 'When I saw there was nothing else for it.'

A week later, when we went to London to buy the ring, Rona and I called in to see Head of Features. She fell for his charm at once, as most people did.

I told him that Dr Barbour had made light of my ills. A long holiday, combined with the swallowing of certain nauseous medicinal draughts in place of whisky, seemed to promise a complete cure.

Then we discussed the dramatized documentary I was going to produce at the end of the year about the life and death of Martin Bormann. By now it was all straight in my head. Police investigation showed that the guesses I'd made while we faced each other on the ledge were generally accurate. MI5 had picked up his trail during the Eichmann trial in Israel, when a prosecution document had been sent from Germany with a pencilled note on the back: *'Bormann to see Rivington-Keel, midday tomorrow.'*

Finally I said: 'I'm afraid this may be the last programme I'll do for you. When all the legal tangles have been straightened out, Rona and I are going to live in Kersivay – in the Big House.'

He twinkled. 'Laird Parsons. Sooner or later I knew it would happen.'

'I think my father would have approved.'

'I know, Peter. And I wish you luck. You deserve it, both of you.' He and Rona exchanged smiles: buddies they were, already. 'At the same time,' he went on, pressing the tips of his fingers together, 'is there any reason why you shouldn't go on doing occasional jobs for us as a freelance? I'm sure a foray from your Hebridean fastness once or twice a year would be an interesting change – not only for you but for your wife.'

'Exactly what I've been telling him,' said Rona. 'He'd soon feel lost without his script conferences and midget tape-recorders. Besides, a hair-do in Kersivay does tend to be rather dicey.'

'Quite. Think it over, Peter. Or do you really need to?'

I didn't, of course. I'd have hated depriving the announcers of their tongue-twister, 'Produced by Peter Parsons'.

A good old scout, the Laughing Cavalier.